LOVE OF MY LIVES

RIVER DANIEL

CHANGE OF HEART PRESS
SALEM, SOUTH CAROLINA

3rd edition

ISBN-13: 978-0-9881784-6-5

DEDICATION

To my sons for believing in me

and
my husband who did not know what he was getting himself
into when he married a writer.

*This book is a work of fiction. Any resemblance to persons
living or dead is probably well thought out.*

ACKNOWLEDGEMENTS

My editor and friend, Sandy Rankin,
who made it so much better.

ONE—BRENDA

Emily stared at the words. Effortlessly, almost, the typewritten story about Brenda had appeared on the pages without her questioning from where it came.

```
            DESTINY'S WAY
   A SHORT STORY BY EMILY MASON

I remember being murdered. I died in
1865, a terrifying, violent death. I
shall never forget it.
   My name was Brenda Callahan. I
lived in Chetco, a coastal town in
southern Oregon, near what is now
Brookings. Life there today consists
of game fishing and whale watching.
```

It was not always so.

My wealthy Irish aunt virtually built the cliffside town, notorious for its gambling casino and lavish upstairs rooms. It disappeared after my death. Aunt Jessee would die of a broken heart, and along with her, the town of Chetco.

As though it were yesterday, I remember my aunt, Jessee McClannahan O'Riley, scurrying about the parlor of our suite in her hotel She fluffed blue velvet pillows and tweaked white crocheted doilies, like an old maid anticipating her first gentleman caller.

"You behave as though a king is coming," I said.

"You just sit yourself and don't be messing up that beautiful dress," she answered, her soft, round and ample form imposing, white hair shimmering, starlight blue eyes twinkling. Still beautiful, though sixty-seven, she wore black taffeta with graceful elegance, an obvious New York transplant, quite unlike the other pioneer women in the area.

The blue organza dress she'd ordered from San Francisco last year for my eighteenth birthday had ruffles at the throat. I wore a cameo of ivory set into Wedgwood—a gift from one of Aunt Jessee's admirers. It made my neck appear even longer.

Every time I protested all the fuss she shushed me, and I obediently refolded my hands in my lap. She punctuated every other sentence with "Listen, Luv." I liked it when she called me Luv.

"Listen, Luv, this Bond Bartello fellow is from an influential family in St. Louis, and we need for him to settle in Chetco," she told me for the hundredth time.

Bond Bartello, heir to the Bartello Imports whiskey importing empire, was scouting expansion locations. I was being used as bait.

I tried to explain that I understood Chetco's need for commerce, but she was too fidgety to listen. I truly did understand. I was well educated and rather sophisticated, thanks to all the books on the shelves that lined our parlor walls. At her insistence, Aunt Jessee's mining friends brought books on their way through Chetco, where good food and clean beds awaited them. But not romance. Aunt Jessee's past prompted her to keep me far away from most men. Now here she was, pushing one on me—and me on him.

"I'm in no hurry to get married, and I might not like him," I said.

She thumped an askew lampshade and

replied, "Listen, Luv, he's rich and handsome, and he has beautiful white teeth. You know how I am about teeth. And you, Brenda Callahan, young lady of marriageable age, do not need to be reminded of the shortage of proper suitors around these parts."

I wanted to be a newspaperwoman, maybe even work in San Francisco, but she always said it was too dangerous. I knew she was right—not about San Francisco being dangerous—but about getting to San Francisco. Stories about Indians attacking stagecoaches reached us regularly. Indians had killed my mother and father, Mathilde and John Callahan. I wound up living with Aunt Jessee, who in 1811 had come to America from Ireland when she was only thirteen, and my mother was a baby.

"That old ship lurched like a buckin' whale trying to disembogue its innards," Aunt Jessee had said, telling the story.

Her head would rock, side to side, remembering her own mother dying while giving birth to my mum. Afterward, my grandfather boarded a ship bound for the new land with his two little daughters, Aunt Jessee and her baby sister Mathilde.

"Poppa and me and your sweet mother, just a baby she was, we got on

4

this big ol' ship that stunk to high heaven, even before the storms started. But that last one, the storm that killed Poppa, was a dilly. Me, crouched under a timber, clutching Mathilde, trying to peer through lightning-blinded eye slits at boxes and bodies flying about.Yessiree, it was a dilly."

The way Aunt Jessee told it I could hear that old hull whimpering and creaking like it was pleading to God for mercy, passengers screaming for help.

"I could hear Poppa calling me, but I could not reach him," she said. "Then his cries stopped, and I knew that somewhere inside that bloody, stinking chaos he was dead."

Aunt Jessee also knew that, somehow, as a thirteen-year-old penniless orphan alone in New York City, she would have to take care of Mathilde.

"If the only way back to Ulster were by sea, Mathilde and I would just have to make it in the New World," she said. "I was not about to step aboard another ship."

Survivors from the shipwreck took Jessee and Mathilde to an orphanage in New York City. Two years later, when she was only fifteen, Aunt Jessee was put out to serve a family she

described as "the batty O'Rileys."
That's when she and my mother got
separated.

I looked at the picture of my
mother, Mathilde, kept on the lace-
covered, round oak table in the
parlor. I liked to think I favored
her—slim, with the same sparkling
green eyes, long neck, wavy, honey-
colored hair and creamy skin. I could
always sense that talking about how
hard it was reminded Aunt Jessee of
how much strength she really had. It
made her feel happy to believe she had
passed some of that strength on to me.
I wonder if she knew how badly I would
need it.

In 1815, seventeen-year-old Jessee
wed the middle O'Riley son, the
addlepated John. Right away, they
produced a baby daughter, Alice.

Four years after the beautiful
young Jessee married John he died,
which Jessee swore was from his
mother's badgering. John's death
caused Mrs. O'Riley to cast Jessee
out—all the while thrusting
insinuations about Alice's parentage.
The woman had been sure that the
lovely Jessee could not love such a
weakling as John, and she had
practiced continual breast-beating
over consenting to the marriage in the
first place. Inevitably, she outright

accused Jessee of betrayal and threw her and four-year-old Alice out of the house on St. John's Square.

Aunt Jessee, determined to prove Mrs. O'Riley right—maybe she was a born whore—vowed she and Alice would not end up in the Five Points district, an odious, noisome, squalid home to hooligans and prostitutes. She spent her only money for a room at the Columbian Hotel on Mulberry Street.

Aunt Jessee told me about the mornings she strolled with Alice through the markets, listening to the shouts of fishmongers, chimney sweeps and peddlers, watching ladies from the fine houses on Lower Second Avenue and Stuyvesant Square all dressed in cloaked cottons scurrying among wagons heaped with venison, squab, and wild boar, accompanied by servants who, Aunt Jessee said, were always either black or Irish.

Her money gone, Aunt Jessee moved to Holy Ground, the area around St. Paul's Church, filled with taverns and houses of prostitution. Proudful stories told by sick old women about the glory days of the Revolution, some forty years previous, convinced Jessee of their contribution to the battle effort, and educated her about the ways of men. Among these women, she found friends to help with little

Alice while Astors draped her in silk and furs. She saved her money to carry out her plan.

In 1825, Jessee took nine-year-old Alice to the newly erected house on the north side of Washington Square, overlooking the parade grounds of the New York State National Guard. Jessee and Alice took up residence alongside families of social status and position, and where generals of the French Revolution would later be welcomed in graciousness and splendor. During the following thirteen years, Aunt Jessee earned and accepted her title, "The Madam of Fifth Avenue."

But life changed when Alice died of cholera at age sixteen.

For six years, Jessee's spirit was restless. Alice's death made her lose her enthusiasm for the city. Since 1836, New York had buzzed with news of The Reverend Marcus Whitman and his wife Narcissa crossing the Rocky Mountains and living to tell about it. Jessee longed for new adventure, confident that wilderness and hostile Indians could not equal the ferocity of storms at sea—or French generals— and she was sufficiently saturated with the opulence of New York City. As she put it, at times she feared she would drown in it.

Aunt Jessee said a golden street

had called her by name in a
premonitory dream, but the street was
very far away. She might even have to
build it herself when she got there.
Jessee joined an ox-drawn Conestoga
caravan and headed west. It took
twelve wagons to carry her belongings.
People thought she was mad because the
lack of passable roads beyond St.
Louis made the eight-month journey
seem impossible. Jessee always said
that one of her claims to fame was
that Ambrose Boone, grandson of
Daniel, shared her vision, and he
found for her men brave enough to
drive her wagons. She was forty years
old and eager to begin again, but she
was leaving New York without ever
having shared her good fortune with my
mother, Mathilde, and about that she
felt guilty.

Jessee arrived in San Francisco
about ten years before the Gold Rush,
with callused hands and all traces of
the city temporarily rattled, rumbled,
and bounced out of her. There she met
and followed John Sutter, who was
building his fort at the site of what
is now Sacramento. Then, J.F. Wendell
came along, and Jessee migrated north
to Crescent City. When she was ready
to build her dream, Jessee set out for
Chetco, where she would stay put.

I was ten years old. It had taken

seventeen years for Jessee to locate us and persuade my mother and father to join her in Chetco. But Indians attacked and killed almost everybody in our caravan. I survived by playing dead. Somebody found me and took me to Aunt Jessee. She took me in, and I took Alice's place as her daughter.

The golden street in the dream turned out to be a hotel she built. Jessee's place became a sanctuary for shipwrecked sailors and sea captains, and any other visitors brave enough to risk the journey to Chetco—such as Bond Bartello.

A sudden tap, tap, tap and swishing black taffeta drew my eyes toward the front door. In walked Mr. Evans, the town banker, and his charge, supposed paragon of virtue and potential citizen of Chetco, Bond Bartello.

Bond Bartello's black eyes glowed as Aunt Jessee introduced me as the light of her life, her only niece, Miss Brenda Callahan. Obviously, Mr. Evans and Aunt Jessee had said more to me about Bond Bartello than they had said to him about me. Perhaps he would flee before he was lassoed and hog-tied, but he was looking at me, as though I were the first woman he had ever seen. I knew he wasn't going anywhere.

And he surely did have excellent

teeth. I liked nice teeth too.

I poured claret and made small talk about their carriage ride out Coast Road to see the view from the cliffs. Bond kept his eyes on me as he assured Mr. Evans and Aunt Jessee that St. Louis surely had nothing like that. I noticed his beautifully tailored suit and fine leather boots and was glad his hat was western, black with a wide faille band, not Derby. I hated Derby hats. I thought they made all men look dumpy.

Amidst talk of fresh sea air, glorious trees, and the latest shipwreck, my feeling grew that there was something peculiar about a man such as Bartello wanting to leave his family and St. Louis. He must have something to hide—or he was running away from something. I knew I was being set up, used as bait to lure new money to Chetco.I decided to be a willing victim in this conspiracy because of Bond's gentlemanly manners and dark good looks. Underneath that polished, relaxed exterior was an intensity I wanted better to understand.

Not totally naive I did do some checking, just not enough.

I telegraphed the *St. Louis Tribune* for any stories on file about this Mr. Bond Bartello, age 32. The only information I could get, Bond explained away satisfactorily.

The telegram said he had been questioned in connection with the suspicious deaths of a Thomas W. Lawton and a woman who turned out to be Bond's former fiancée, Miss Ann Barton. The piece was dated September 9, 1859, only a few months before. He must have left St. Louis shortly afterward. I was surprised to learn he had been engaged to be married, but such a good-looking man would be a prize catch for anyone, I supposed. So after hearing his side of the story, on July 5, 1860, nine weeks after we met, I became Brenda Callahan Bartello.

His side of the story was that witnesses had overheard him threaten to kill Lawton during a fight, in which he had thoroughly thrashed Lawton for insulting Miss Barton. Bond said it had all been a big mistake, that the killer had been caught, and that his engagement had ended long before Miss Barton had been killed. I let it go.

Before the wedding, Bond had also explained away the Mexican, his companion, whom I had loathed on sight. Aunt Jessee had said he must be some sort of servant because Bond had paid to have a hotel room next to his.

I was relieved when Bond said the man had moved on, probably to Astoria, and wouldn't be back. But he did come back.

Our courtship had been short and polite, with less passion than one might expect, and no real conflict. After we had married, we moved into Aunt Jessee's house on the edge of town, which she had built to live in while the hotel was being finished. French blue paper flocked with white feathers perfectly matched the white lace curtains draped over blue window shades brought with her from New York. Later, she'd had black leather furniture hauled out. The rooms were charming and suitable.

During the first few months of matrimony, Bond treated me tenderly, and he was a thoughtful, if infrequent, lover. My only real complaint was that business frequently called him to Port Orford, but I had known about that possibility before I married him, so I didn't gripe. However, one morning the Mexican suddenly appeared at our doorway, asking for Bond. I cringed at his gleaming, devil eyes. He was slimy and smelled awful. His twisted, contemptuous face repulsed me. Apparently, he liked me no better.

"Bond, I came to see Bond," the

Mexican growled.

"He isn't here and won't be back until . . . I don't know when," I said, shooing him away with my hand as though he were a stray animal.

By the time Bond had returned from Port Orford, I had shrugged off my concerns and had attributed my paranoia about the Mexican's fiendish demeanor to an active imagination. Bond was such a gentleman.

Then one day I was busy at Chetco's weekly newspaper, the *Curry Clarion,* and I happened to glance out the window and catch sight of Bond leaving the hotel. Before I could call to him, the Mexican, who had been standing in the alley, beckoned Bond to come over to him. Bond complied, and I watched as they conversed quietly. It was obvious they were trying to prevent their voices from being overheard.

The Mexican appeared pernicious, Bond contrite. The contrast between them was ludicrous but frightening: Bond, so immaculate, so fastidious; the Mexican, a malevolent jackal. I could not begin to fathom this unlikely alliance between my husband and this noxious barbarian.

The Curry Clarion editor, Jim Johnstone, interrupted my observations. Jim agreed with me that the Mexican was strange.

"He more or less comes and goes, and it is understood that he works for Bond," Jim said.

"Some may understand it, but not me."

"You look pale, Brenda. Are you feeling well?" Jim said.

Jim had always tried to hide his feelings for me because he was so much older and very shy. But whenever he felt deeply about anything, he feigned indifference by chewing on a pencil. He was shredding a pencil to pieces with his teeth, pieces of it hanging from his mustache. He resembled a walrus.

"I'm pregnant," I said, matter-of-factly.

Jim was such a good friend that I felt no remorse telling him I was pregnant even before I told Bond. When I did tell Bond, he seemed happy enough, but I saw a shadow cross his face. I know now he was probably worried about breaking the news to the Mexican.

One night in bed, I pressed Bond about him.

"Bond, that Mexican slinks around like a coyote. He's just dreadful, and I want him to stay away from the house."

"He doesn't lurk, and why don't you use his name? His name is Jose," Bond said. "I suppose he feels indebted because I tried to help his family back in St. Louis. I pulled his brothers out of a fire. He probably feels grateful," he added.

I knew there was more to it, and *no thank you very much I had no intention of using the Mexican's name as if he were a real person.* But Bond's visible discomfort at being questioned silenced me. I saw a barely perceptible clench mark his fist and jaw, and I felt afraid of his anger.

I tried to let it go, but why was Bond evading the issue? And if the Mexican loved Bond out of gratitude for some noble act, why did he hate me? And if Bond rescued his brothers from a fire, why wasn't that in the St. Louis papers? Surely, he didn't mean the big fire in '49. And why didn't he mention the fire when I asked the first time? I knew I wouldn't be able to let it rest. I'd have to have a better explanation, one that I believed.

When our beautiful baby daughter, Jennifer LeAndrea Bartello, was born in that big birch and brass bed, on July 12, 1861, Bond was hysterical and utterly useless. Aunt Jessee told me later that she had never seen a grown man more excited or more helpless over one little baby.

Love of My Lives

While I was in labor, I could hear Bond's black leather boots clumping across the oak floors as he paced back and forth.

"During practically your entire labor, Bond was holding a glass of bourbon so tightly I thought at any moment it would shoot straight up out of his hand, like a squeezed fish," Aunt Jessee said.

When Bond saw Jenny for the first time, he cried.

"I never thought this could happen to me," he said.

I wondered why such a handsome man felt that way. Now, of course, I know. That horrible Mexican.

When Jenny was two, Bond was on one of his trips, and I had left her with Mrs. James, a neighbor. It was unusually hot and dry. Rain would wash the town clean eventually, but not this day. This day was the beginning of the end for Jenny, as it turned out, for me too.

His name was Emil Chevalier.

I'll never forget those four brown horses choking on that cloud of dust, and the stagecoach rattling to a halt in front of Aunt Jessee's hotel. When Emil stepped out of the stagecoach, I could feel his power from forty feet away. He was a vision of cultured, elegant maleness, shining like gold among the miners. He was not especially tall, but his clothes were cut to define his broad-shouldered leanness. Before I could find out anything else about him, Jimmy James came running through the door, shouting that his mother had sent him to tell me to come quickly. "Baby Jenny don't seem right!" he yelled.

When I arrived at the James' house, my precious Jenny lay feverish, ashen, and sweating. I sat cradling her in my arms, waiting for Dr. Benson, stroking her damp black curls and kissing the lids of her blue eyes, which were streaking with orange and yellow. Her normally pink skin was turning gray and feeling cold and clammy. She tried to say "Mommie," but she was too weak to speak.

"A cholera outbreak down in Ft. Sutter is moving northward. The town will have to be quarantined," Doc Benson said when he arrived.

But Jenny and dozens of other children died, and Bond took it as hard as I did, as did Aunt Jessee, who relived her own Alice's death all over again.

Something in me just turned cold inside, and I could not feel anything at all.

One day some weeks later, I was back at the newspaper and in through the door walked Emil Chevalier.

Maybe if Jenny had not died, maybe what happened next would not have happened. I'll never know. But Emil's gentle way of offering his condolences and apologizing for the imposition captivated my imagination, which, I suppose, was desperately seeking diversion from the grief of losing Jenny. When he reached out and touched my hand, I found myself surrendering my grief to his gentleness, feeling his amber eyes filling my emptiness. It was as though honey-colored light nourished my soul. I marveled at how his touch could give me peace when nothing Bond had said or tried to do had helped. At the thought of Bond, I felt guilt and shame. He had suffered as great a loss as I. But in that moment, my future was being set by a choice I didn't even know I was making.

When Bond's business trips resumed, I was glad. I made no effort to hide my feelings for Emil from Aunt Jessee or Jim Johnstone. Both were wild with worry about what Bond would do if he found out I was carrying on.

Bond had been drinking since Jenny's death. Jessee warned me about pushing Bond's temper, which was growing meaner with every drink. But Bond never confronted me about my feelings for Emil. If he felt tortured, I was indifferent to his feelings. Now that Jenny was dead I cared for nothing but Emil, who was so very different from Bond.

Unlike Bond, who had been secretive from the beginning, Emil spoke freely of his life and travels throughout the New World researching the music of this new land. His parents in France had hoped he would become a musician, but instead, his first love was words. Words' music, he said, fulfilled his need to create. And he fulfilled my need to love.

The first night I took him into Bond's bed, as shamelessly as a Fifth Avenue whore, I laughed when his shoes hit the floor. I had never laughed with Bond. Emil and I thought we would spend eternity together. And maybe we will. Only time will tell.

One afternoon we packed a picnic and rode out to the cliffs, by way of the Coast Road. To the south, the cliffs were jagged, steep and dangerous. To the north, they sloped gently downward to the Pacific, quieter this day than at times.

A romantic cove of dry sand at low tide beckoned as we descended the boulders like two children at play, giggling, trying not to frighten the brown seals languishing on a rock, sunning themselves six-hundred feet out into the water. The waves absorbed the sounds of our laughter; the seals merely grunted, turned their heads away from two silly humans, and went back to sleep.

In the cove, feeling sheltered and hidden from prying eyes, we helped each other spread the blanket on the sand and laid out fresh sourdough bread, red wine, and a soft, white cheese. But fresh-born passion erased any hunger we had for anything but each other. There was little need to speak. We had said it all. Yes, I would marry him. Yes, I would live in Paris. Yes, I would leave next week.

We stripped each other naked and made love in the sunlight. I realize now what a daring thing we did. It did not seem so at the time. It just felt right. Afterward, I thought I heard horses' hooves in the distance, galloping away.

A few days later, a soft knock on my door drew me onto the porch. There stood the malodorous Mexican, gravely solemn, his voice raspy and low.

"Bond has been hurt in a rock slide. You come with me," he demanded and grabbed my arm. His gruff manner left me neither time to reason, nor any recourse except to go with him. Resigned that Bond needed me, I climbed into the rickety wagon beside the Mexican. Repulsed by his odor, I leaned as far away from him as possible and demanded to know how badly Bond was hurt. But he would only snarl, then whip the horse faster.

Knots of fear gripped my stomach, the Mexican's churlishness feeding waves of terror rushing down the sides of my neck into my fingertips clutching the sides of the wobbling wagon, now bouncing wildly over the rocky Coast Road, the frantic horse racing to outrun the whip.

In my hysteria, thoughts of rushing headlong over the cliffs and meeting Jenny in the sky almost made me laugh. Suddenly, though, the horizon became visible, and he jerked the horse southward.

Over my right shoulder, a hundred feet straight down the sheer rock face, crashing waves came into view. Flailing the air with my fists I screamed, "Tell me where Bond is!" But the wagon's swaying, clamoring rattle and the frightened horse's thundering hooves made it almost impossible to grasp what he was shouting over the raging noise.

". . . you wenches are all alike. You claim to love Bond, but no one loves him but me. With you dead, I will have him to myself!" he screamed.

Then he slowed the horse, and I could hear him better.

" . . . Barton bitch claimed to love him too, but she got pregnant by Lawton. I killed them both."

Mockingly he was confessing to murdering a pregnant woman, as well as her lover. Then I realized he could not be planning to let me live if he was telling me this.

His sudden blow to my left shoulder knocked me out of the wagon. He jumped down behind me.

"Now you will die as well!" he shouted. Then he kicked me.

I tumbled toward the cliff, wildly grasping onto rocks with my hands, trying to keep myself from falling. Rocks slashed my skin, and cliff winds blew my dress up over my face, smothering me. The next thing I knew he was wrenching my bleeding hands loose from the jagged, jutting stone to which I clung. He yanked me up by my forearms and dangled me over the edge of the cliff.

I still feel his grip on my arms and the spray of his spittle on my face and the sight of his ocher teeth growing into fangs in my fright-shocked mind, as I heard him utter, "Bond . . . I do as Bond wishes."

He turned loose of my forearms and roared over the howling wind, "Drown, wench, drown!"

Then he dropped me over the edge of
the cliff.

My soul slipped out of my body and
hovered briefly, watching my body
falling and smashing onto the boulders
below, the bloody hem of my dress
slowly disappearing beneath the
churning waves.

The end.

TWO—EMILY

Emily stared at the last graf of the story she had just written about Brenda. Where did *that* come from. It wasn't a question. She pushed her hands against her desk, still staring at the page in her typewriter. A dream about a jackal holding her head under water flickered at the edges of her mind, like the jagged lights of an ocular migraine. *Time is short. Concert starts at eight o'clock. I'd better get dressed.*

From the closet, Emily chose the new white iridescent dress she had purchased off the runway in Dallas during the last Fashion Week she had covered for the paper. She had saved it for something special. It would do nicely tonight for Yo-Yo Ma.

Red velvet curtains concealed the stage of the

smaller, more intimate of the two theaters in the Water's Edge Music Hall. Behind the curtains, from time to time, great entertainers awaited. Tonight it was internationally acclaimed, a 23-year-old cellist, Yo-Yo Ma.

Emily sat with her husband, Jason Wohl, third-row center, compliments of Yo-Yo Ma himself, their hands, mouths and minds quiet, but not peaceful.

Jason and Emily co-owned the *Water's Edge Daily News.* Anyone watching would see an affluent, attractive couple who shared nothing else but the paper. They sat stiffly, looking straight ahead at the chair legs peeking out from beneath the velvet. Joint ownership of the paper meant practically nothing to their marriage. Jason, as publisher, tended to the business end. Emily wrote editorials and sometimes features, but interviewing entertainment greats playing the condo circuit was a perk she reserved for herself. She had written a story for the paper about Yo-Yo Ma's appearance on the Gulf Coast of Florida, and he had left tickets at the box office for her. She had donated her regular season tickets to the cello students at the Water's Edge Conservatory of Music.

Sparkling chandeliers twittered above the rows of sloping seats, filled with dressed-to-the-*nines* transplanted Yankees, snowbirds, retirees, and vacationers. Everyone welcomed the holiday season, a chance to dress up for a change, dirty sneakers, cutoffs, and t-shirts being the norm for most of the locals.

Not Emily. She liked wearing white year-round, no matter how impractical it was in her work, which sometimes included getting dirty supporting her best friend, Marta Miller, Water's Edge City Prosecutor. Just last week they unofficially schlocked around Sawgrass County, looking for a farm recently bought by the Christionologists, a pseudo-religious group that was buying up all the buildings in Water's Edge, threatening to decimate the city's tax base. Now it seemed city property was not enough. They were spreading out into surrounding counties.

Footsteps behind the curtain. Deep tone from a cello string. Rattling chains lifting the heavy crimson. The magical maestro, looking young and handsome in his black tuxedo, dark eyes shining, smiled, bowed, said hello, sat down and began to play the gleaming instrument.

Jason gently touched Emily's arm, signaling his approval. Jason never needed an excuse to dress up. Emily complained to Marta he would wear a suit and tie to bed if he could get away with it. Emily patted his hand, resigned to Jason's obsession with upholding his dignified professional image. He had been this way the whole twelve years they had known each other. They met when he was the advertising director for a newspaper in Gainesville, and she was a cub reporter. They married two years later, and Jason had been the most unimaginative, infrequent lover ever since.

"It's as though he does not know what to do!" Emily wailed to Marta one night when they worked late and out of exhaustion drifted into woman talk. "Sometimes he seems to want me, but other times it seems he only wants to want me, but he doesn't. Not really, you know. It's like he's got this big secret."

During intermission, Emily left Jason chatting with people in row three while she wandered in search of libation. Concertgoers, body to body, ordered cocktails from the bar set up in the lobby. Emily succeeded in procuring a Scotch, then tried to make her way to the door. Her hand touched the door handle at the same moment as his. They looked at each other, and looked at each other, and looked at each other, and looked at each other.

Embarrassing.

Then they silently pushed their way outside into the fresh evening breeze.

"The concert is going well," Emily mumbled self-consciously, eyes averted but trying to hold the Scotch with one hand while clutching her breeze-blown tresses with the other. She would later tell Marta she felt like an idiot dwarf, her five feet, five inches stopping about mid-way up his chest. She let her eyes travel upward to meet his again, to be sure, certain of the color. Amber. Black hair and amber eyes. She felt a buzz that she was pretty sure was not the Scotch.

"Yo-Yo Ma is a genius," he said, looking directly at the diamond band on Emily's left hand.

Emily didn't respond. Instead she touched her forehead with the icy cup of Chivas, trying to quell the vibration that was making her feel faint. Intensely aware that he was noticing the way the iridescent white beaded dress clung to her hips.

"I'm sorry for being so presumptuous," he said. "I see by your ring that you are married, but I feel compelled to tell you I have never seen anyone so beautiful."

Emily gasped, shocked and flustered, and dropped the Chivas, splattering golden droplets of Scotch onto his shoes as it hit the ground.

He jumped back, startled. "I am so sorry. I don't know what got into me. I never move that fast. Blame it on vacationitis. Do you have a card in that tiny little purse?" he said.

"I, uh . . . no, sorry," she said, digging into the only pocket inside her sparkly evening bag.

"My name is Emily Mason." She dropped the hyphenated Wohl from her name. "I'm a columnist for the *Water's Edge Daily News*. My husband Jason and I own the paper."

"Jason Mason?"

"No, no. Jason Wohl. I'm sorry. I write under Emily Mason. My cards say Emily Mason hyphen Wohl. But I don't seem to have one," she said, digging fiercely into the bottom of the evening bag. "At any rate, it's the little paper in Water's Edge. The big paper is in Tampa."

She glanced up at him long enough to ask, "And you are?"

Oh, good Lord, my face is so hot I must look like a strawberry.

"Alessio Giles Lavalle, Music Critic, *Boston Times*. I'm reviewing for the paper," he said. "Thought I might as well make the vacation tax deductible."

Emily memorized his grin, dimples, and white teeth. "They're flashing the lights. We'd better go in."

"Ok, but I owe you a Scotch."

"Promise?"

"Name the time and place," he said.

She easily walked underneath his arm as he held the heavy glass door for her.

Back inside, Emily never heard another note Yo-Yo Ma played. Squirming, uncomfortable, the plush red velour beneath her offered no consolation for her increasing agitation.

Dear God, help me.

Energized, electrified, fearful.

Where is this coming from?

She pressed her fingers into the pit of her stomach, as though she could push out a troubling anxiety originating from somewhere so deeply within she could not identify its origin.

"Are you all right?" said Jason.

"Enthralled," she said, a bit more sardonically than she had intended, feeling foolish for feeling so much about a stranger, just because he said something nice. But was he a stranger? She did not know. Something unsettling, familiar, about the intensity of this emotion, the sort of thing that leads to trouble.

I'm glad he moved so fast. I was thinking the same thing about him. Beautiful. No ring.

She was glad she was not reviewing, as he was. The thought of Alessio's low mellow voice filled her ears, and the awareness of his presence in the theater filled the rest of her. She moved her head neither left nor right for fear she would see him and give herself away.

Is he the one in my journal?

He owes me a Scotch.

Her heart was making music at the thought of seeing Alessio again. And she knew she would.

Nothing would stand in destiny's way

THREE—EMILY and MARTA

The path down to the harbor ran alongside a thick planting of holly shrubs that obligingly covered themselves in red berries just in time to help celebrate the holidays. The library groundskeeper placed poinsettia pots every two feet and strung red tinsel garlands down the handrail. He had to get started early because it was his job to make sure everything was finished before the snowbirds' families began arriving the week before Thanksgiving. It all looked out of place against the natural beauty of sunlight dancing between the boats in the harbor. Even they were decorated, red and green streamers fluttering in the wind. Emily and Marta paid them no mind.

"A letter came to the paper this morning," said Emily, "from the Cadillac dealer, accusing the Chrions of ruining his business because people won't come downtown as long as they are here, marching around in those long white robes, proselytizing."

"Is Eddy going to print it?" said Marta.

Whitecaps decorated the bay waters. Halyards clanged against masts, as nearby merchants, armed with cans of fake snow, waited for the breezes to subside so they could decorate the outside of their windows.

"You know Eddy. He brought it up again how grateful he is that Jason has remained silent about them. Their promises of redeveloping the downtown could mean a lot of new business for the paper."

"Try explaining that to the Cadillac dealer. Now they're charging the city with religious persecution," said Marta, stopping to inhale the fresh salty air. "Judge Ryder ordered them to pay four hundred twenty thousand dollars in back property taxes, but they own fifteen percent of the city real estate now, worth more than ten million dollars. The State Attorney is looking at their application for tax exemption, hoping to find false information he can prove."

"Yes, Eddy told me," said Emily, following Marta's lead and breathing deeply.

"I can't imagine Eddy, of all managing editors, ever letting business dictate editorial policy," said Marta.

"It's the secrecy."

"Did the mayor really call them cretins and mental cripples to their faces the other night?"

"Yep. That's what Sal said. He covers commission meetings," said Emily. "Is the mayor still packing a gun?"

"Bullet-proof vest, too," said Marta, plucking a red berry from a holly bush.

"What about the new regulations against charitable solicitation inside city limits?"

"Lawyers screaming about Constitutional rights, that's what about it," said Marta. "Of course, that bit about going to jail for deceiving donors may help. But really, what's one more lawsuit."

"True. They'll just go back to their congregation and say God said for them to give, give, give…"

"…or Angler will be called to heaven." The women giggled.

"Just think if the whole three million of them chip in a dollar a day. No wonder they can afford hotels and yachts. Just look at that thing sitting down there in the harbor. Darn thing looks like the Queen Mary."

"Well, not really, but this sleepy little town's never seen anything like it," said Emily.

They reached their favorite bench underneath a huge water oak that covered half a city block in the deliciously welcome shade, even in the wintertime.

"Sit."

Marta obeyed.

"Have you been to the beach without me? You look tan," said Emily.

"Nah. Ham and I hung out by the pool this weekend."

"I like your hair color. What is that?"

"Burnished tabac," said Marta. "Loreal. New color."

"It brings out your big brown eyes. Nice with your tan. How many times have you changed it now? Fifteen?"

"Well, if I had your shiny dark locks I wouldn't have to keep changing it. I just realized…you're not covering up your freckles with makeup."

"Well, if I had your beautiful bronze body I wouldn't have freckles. Alessio likes them."

"Thanks. Is Eddy still mad about the lack of reaction to the takeover story?"

"Certainly. He expected anger and panic. Instead, he got a big yawn from John Q. Public."

"Even with FBI documents to back it up?"

"Nobody believes they want to own it all. Office buildings, hospitals, police, even the state attorney's office."

"Would that make Angler my boss?" Marta made a face. Emily laughed.

"What have you found out about the farm up in Sawgrass County?" Emily said.

"This much we know . . . two crop dusters reported seeing a couple of people running for what seemed to be a door in a hillside, hurrying, like they didn't want to be seen. But when the pilots circled back around, the door had disappeared. All they saw was a grass-covered hill, and, of course, the ever-present sheep," said Marta

"An underground hideaway?"

"Probably. Jurisdiction up there in Sawgrass County is on the table now," said Marta. "Mandino said a couple of babies turned up dead up there. Don't know if there's a connection."

Emily scrubbed her nails up and down her arms. "That makes my skin crawl."

"I have to get back to work. Alessio has asked me to go away with him this weekend," Emily said, watching Marta's square jaw for the set that would mean she disapproved. It did not come.

"After only two weeks? You're making progress with the guilt thing."

"Am I?"

"Apparently. Have you realized how lately you've been giggling?"

"Have I?"

"Incessantly. I'm jealous."

"Good. Maybe you will give Ham the boot and make room for someone terrific, like Alessio."

"He's got good hands."

"So you keep saying."

"Did I tell you Alessio is not from Boston? He was born in New York. Westchester."

"That explains the Italian good looks."

"His mother is French."

"You've learned a lot about him."

"We've talked on the phone every day for two weeks."

"How are you going to get away from Jason?"

"I didn't say I was going."

"What? Even after you think Jason is seeing someone else? Not go?"

"I hope he is. There was just that one phone call in June, but he seems to be disappearing a lot lately."

"Look, you heard him say it had to stop; he couldn't see the person anymore. The lawyer in me says that's evidence."

FOUR—EMILY and ALESSIO

The eastern sky glowed with moonlight shining through large fluffy white clouds rimmed in golden stars. Emily was so nervous she barely noticed, keeping her eyes on the road as she drove down to St. Petersburg Beach.

The Gulf of Mexico lapped softly at the white sands behind the famous blue hotel. There was no reason for them to drive six hours to Fort Lauderdale when a forty-five-minute drive south to St. Petersburg Beach would provide all the privacy they were seeking.

Emily arrived around 8:15 Saturday night and parked the Jaguar among the other Jaguars in the indoor garage. She caught the elevator to the sixth floor, south corner suite Alessio had taken for the weekend. She tapped the door lightly, ignoring her nervousness. She was going through with this. No matter what. Guilt or no guilt.

He opened the door, took her in his arms, and

began kissing her. Eight hours later they were both sitting cross-legged on the bed, watching the moon set over the Gulf of Mexico, illuminating the curve of the earth, the shimmering waters still as a quiet, peaceful lake.

"Moonrise in the eastern sky, moonset in the western sky, and soon sunrise in the eastern sky," said Alessio. "We don't have this in Boston." The love light in his eyes warmed Emily's heart.

Alessio poured them each a glass of champagne. Candlelight seemed redundant.

"Alessio, do you believe in destiny?" said Emily, her voice as quiet as the night. No other sounds reached their ears but the breeze coming in from the balcony. The silver satin slip she wore reflected the moon's glow. The moonglow on her face and eyes reflected love.

He was quiet for a moment. Emily waited silently, drinking in his beauty along with a sip of champagne. His dark curly hair, cut touchably short, invited Emily's palms to reach out, but she sat motionless, admiring the way his dark brows corniced the amber-colored, deeply thoughtful eyes.

Finally, he said, "I believe there's a natural law that says if you mix red paint and blue paint you're destined to get purple paint. So if you don't want purple paint, don't mix red and blue.

Why do you ask?" He reached forward and touched Emily's soft, smooth cheek. She marveled at the feel of his hand, comforting, as Jason's had never been.

She wrapped both hands around his and pressed, then said, "Brilliant. Alessio, you're brilliant. That is the perfect explanation for destiny and predestination. Paint cans!"

She stroked his forearm, noting its large size and olive skin, basking in its strength. *What a wonderful arm.*

"Do you believe certain people are meant to be together? That perhaps they were together before?"

"You mean as in a past life?" He took her hand and kissed her palm.

"Yes." She stroked his chin and touched his dimple with the tip of her finger.

"As a matter of fact, I don't have a problem with that idea. Does that surprise you?" he said, pushing her backward onto the pillow. He pulled up her satin slip and kissed her belly.

"A little." She arched upward to push her tummy against his lips.

He stopped kissing her long enough to say "Why?" Then he moved his head lower.

"You know . . . the religious and cultural taboos against anything . . . Eastern." She placed her hands on the top of his head and toyed with his hair.

He looked up. "What are you leading up to?" Then he moved his head even lower.

"It will have to wait."

She let herself relax, and they both stopped talking.

They never slept; before daybreak they made love on the beach. Then they showered and put on white terry robes supplied by the hotel. Room service brought Eggs Benedict and orange juice to go with the coffee. Emily, her hair hidden beneath a white turban, her freckles all scrubbed and clean, smelled like fresh lemon peel from the hotel soap.

"You look adorable," said Alessio, tightening the robe's belt around her waist.

Over breakfast, at a table set with white linen, sterling accouterments and red roses, Emily sank into the lush burgundy chair. "I think I have written about you most of my adult life. May I read you some of it?"

"I'd be honored," he said.

Emily pulled her pink journal out of the straw tote that was waiting on the floor beside her. The memory of her blue journal at home in the closet nagged at her, but she ignored it and began to read:

> *Perhaps I am mad. If I am, my madness is filled with light, hope, and sparkling, twinkling illusions of someday meeting my lost love. All foreboding darkness and doubts, formed by logic, born of*

reason, fed by intellect, vanishes as the flicker of distant love lights my path home. If I stand still, will he come to me? If this is right, will it not just be?

"Go on," Alessio said.

"All right, but first I must say something."

"Go ahead, Baby. Say what is in your heart."

His voice settled her, gave her the courage to speak openly, looking directly at him, finding the words that, once spoken, would forever change her destiny.

"I have never loved Jason. I know that now. I have since the beginning always loved you, Alessio. Only I did not know your name." She lowered her eyes a little surprised at herself. She glanced up in time to see him smile a smile that made her feel she had known him a hundred years. Maybe more.

"Don't you see? I always thought our empty marriage was my fault. If I could love him well enough, everything would be all right. But how could I?" she cried. "I have always loved you, either before I knew you . . . now, or in another life! If so, that would explain . . . I can't blame Jason for being the kind of husband he has been. Who knows how he would have been if he had been truly loved."

"I am with you completely."

"Oh, are you? Are you?"

"Yes, I understand and let me throw this in because it's important. The question of our being together before is an important one. I don't want to break your train of thought, but I want you to know this about me. I am not a religious man, but I do believe…."

"Oh, Alessio, I am so glad. I believe, too!"

"…and my belief tells me that reincarnation becomes unnecessary. But here we are, for whatever reason, and in my heart I know we are meant to be together. Now read."

"Thank you for saying that."

"You're welcome. Read!"

"Ok, ok…I'm reading."

Emily continued, her voice controlled:

When it starts, the 'it' being the feeling that out there, somewhere, he's looking for me too, searching strangers' faces in ticket lines, feeling as foolish as I feel, but feeling driven by the need to find me, as I am him. I try to deny it. When it stops, I grieve its absence, positive it is gone forever, but it never is. It always returns, resurrects, rises from a grave in my mind, shining, light-filled, declaring itself to be my savior, my redeemer, my way home. What would I do if he found me? Would I drop my nets and follow him? To where?

Emily dropped her journal and cried out, "Oh Alessio, to where would I follow you? Boston?"

The horrible thought hit her. Boston isn't far enough away. Another planet would barely be enough space between what she'd be leaving and what she would be walking, running, hurtling toward.

"How much pain can one inflict and survive?" said Emily.

"Wait a minute," said Alessio. "Who says you'd be inflicting pain? How do you know Jason wouldn't rejoice in your departure? Especially if you leave the money."

"Money?"

"Yes, money. I was watching him at the concert. Jason's passion is somewhere else. A man knows these things." He put his hands on her shoulders and looked into her face tenderly.

"I have enough money for both of us. And I don't intend to lose you. Not ever. I'm asking you here and now to leave Jason and marry me."

Momentarily stunned, Emily recovered her senses almost immediately.

"Yes! Yes! Good Heavens, yes! It's what I want! More than anything in this world!"

"I hear a but," said Alessio.

"No, no buts." Emily's mind began racing. "It's just that there was a time when I desperately clung to the illusion that Jason's partnering and mine had produced not only material gains but also intangible joys such as genuine love for others and even us. I desperately wanted to believe that what we had was genuine, absolute, total devotion to one another. I tried to tell myself we'd each given more to each other than any two people I'd ever known."

"What's your point?" said Alessio, amused.

"There surely must be one," Emily said, barely taking a breath and noticing he was trying to hide a wry smile.

"It seemed at times that Jason and I had grown in the ten years we'd been together, even in being able to depend upon each other. For heaven's sake, it wasn't all bad."

Emily stood up, her mind still racing, and began pacing the Persian carpet, first waving her arms then folding them across her chest, hugging herself to keep from knocking over Stiffel lamps, searching for the point of her diatribe.

"I needed to see it as being so beautiful, so safe, so secure, so touching, so true. I told myself we had it all and I would not be disappointed if we lived out our lives together— this time. I believed what I had to."

She stopped, then rushed over to where he was still sitting at the breakfast table, white linen napkin on his lap, arms folded, patiently allowing her to get it out of her system.

"A woman like you would not leave a marriage easily. I understand, Baby."

She dropped to her knees before him, pushed the napkin to the floor, and laid her head upon his bare beautiful muscular thighs. He began stroking the nape of her neck. She picked up the napkin and wiped her tears off his leg.

"Oh, Alessio, if it had been possible to close my eyes and make it happen, I would have wished you away. I would have wrapped your memory in a ribbon and tucked it away on a high shelf, forgotten until it would not hurt anyone to exist. The thought of causing Jason more pain wrenches the core of my being," she said, sniveling and wiping her eyes.

"He seems tortured by some secret. I had resolved to pour all of myself that was humanly possible into this union, at each step of the way asking, what *is* the most loving thing I can do for this man who seems so tortured."

She got up off her knees and continued pacing, her hands thrust deeply into the pockets of the terry robe, searching for a tissue with which to blow her nose, her back turned to him. She gave up and reached for the napkin on the floor.

"Sometimes I would pray. Prayers do not go unanswered. My rational prayers have declared an acceptance—no an *embracing*, of circumstances as they have presented themselves! I have known and willingly acknowledged responsibility for the good and the bad this union has witnessed. I don't know why but I've had to believe that no other could have tried harder nor succeeded more fully!"

"And now? What do you believe now?" Alessio

said, remaining still.

She whirled to face him.

"It was all hogwash! Not the part about wanting it to work, but that it could work just because I wanted it to work. Maybe I have been living a fantasy double life!"

"And now it's over," Alessio said, gently, and stood up. "Baby, come here," he said, and Emily dissolved in the comfort of his arms.

"Listen to me, Emily," he said, holding her carefully, "I realize you don't want to hurt Jason, and I love you all the more for it. You are a sweet spirit, but you must not let your naiveté where Jason is concerned . . . ."

"Naiveté?"

". . . naiveté," he said. "At the concert . . . "

"Oh, Alessio! Could that have been a mere two weeks ago?"

"No wonder you're rattled, but listen to me, Emily. Telling Jason won't be as hard as you think. Trust me. Jason struck me as a realist. He knows the reality of his situation better than you do."

Driving home Emily wondered what Alessio meant by Jason's situation.

FIVE—EMILY'S BLUE JOURNAL

Emily drove home Sunday night, thinking about how her whole life just changed. Alessio had booked a midnight flight back to Boston. An airport limo picked him up.

Emily determined to tell Jason the truth. She and Alessio planned a life together. She had not even bothered to cover her tracks by filling her car with phony shopping bags. Keep it clean. Tell the truth. It will either work out or it won't.

Within thirty minutes of arriving home, I will tell him, and it will be done, and I will be on the phone to Marta.

Emily imagined herself saying, "Marta, I need you. Meet me in the park tomorrow. I just told Jason I am leaving him."

"Must've been a helluva weekend," Marta would say. "How did he take it?"

"He did not even seem surprised," Emily would

say. "He seemed to be expecting it, just like Alessio said he would."

Jason was not at home.

Emily went to her closet to retrieve the blue journal, hidden behind a row of boots. It was not there.

She supposed it did not matter much now anyway. The truth would be out soon.

Wouldn't it?

Where is Jason?

Emily prepared to sleep in the loft, in case Jason returned home before morning. She could not very well go back to their bed after the time she just spent with Alessio. She hid her pink journal inside the slit in the lining of her purse, a trick she learned in college for hiding cigs from her snoopy roommates.

SIX—JASON'S SECRET

Jason watched Emily back her white Jaguar out of the driveway of their two hundred thousand dollar glorified duplex. He liked the view of the golf course. Professional tennis players stayed in the model on the corner whenever they were playing tournaments at the club. Jason and Emily had lived in one of the neighborhood homes, but it was too much upkeep for busy professionals. These were not condo units because owners purchased the land underneath them. Emily had put in a heated, private pool, and the homes all had private two-car garages.

They were PUDs, planned unit developments, meaning they all looked alike, and everything had to be approved by the neighborhood board before so much as a different bush could be planted.

Fort Lauderdale to do some Christmas shopping, she'd said. Wanted to leave Saturday night to get an early start on Sunday sales. Jason waited long enough to be sure she wouldn't return because she'd forgotten something, then picked up the phone.

He dialed a number, then up hung up before the phone on the other end started ringing. He turned his back on the telephone as though it were a hideous thing. *Hideous*. But irresistible. Like Alfredo.

He dialed again.

"It's me," he said when the familiar voice on the other end of the line answered.

"Ja-son, *mi amor*, you come, hey? You meet me at our usual place, hey, and you bring money, hey, amigo? The caddy needs a brake job, man. Come on. I see you in about an hour. I do it for you, Ja-son. *Mi amante*."

After Jason had hung up the phone, he went straight out into the garage and fired up his black Cadillac. He had bought three yellow ones for Alfredo in years past.

Jason's millions came from his only uncle when he died. His self-loathing made him think about not opening the garage door. *Just let the car run long enough and it would be all over.* But he didn't have the courage.

He pushed the button on the remote door opener, backed the car out, and slowly eased out of the neighborhood to meet his lover.

The moon was rising out of the east when he arrived at a sleazy motel on Tampa's Dale Mabry Highway.

SEVEN—EMILY'S DECISION

Monday noon, the Water's Edge Library Park teemed with Christmas shoppers needing a place to rest their feet after walking all over town buying gifts for loved ones up North. Not even the Chrions could scare them away, despite the assertions of the local merchants. The weather was an accommodating seventy-four degrees, and the humidity was down to sixty percent. Such days were made for lovers, and many sprawled on the lush green grass, some on blankets, some on the lawn itself, uncaring for anything except blue skies and each other.

Sailing yachts, large and small, awaited the opening of the drawbridge, visible from the bench where Emily and Marta sat, changing shoes, replacing high heels with sneakers.

"Alessio is in Boston. Left last night. Moving to Florida."

"Must've been a helluva weekend."

"And Jason's missing in action."

"Good timing, I guess," said Marta, relaxing her body onto the stone bench. "So, tell me about your weekend."

Emily pressed both hands against the bench's coolness and rocked herself forward and backward, her toes curling upward at the memory of Alessio's lovemaking.

"Remember all those poems and fantasies I've written about finding a lost love?"

"You mean the ones you thought were maybe 'mythical, romantic, yet archetypal images, which live in the hearts of all women?' Those?"

"Yeah, those."

"All true, huh?"

"Yep."

Emily and Marta hugged each other, whooping and laughing so loudly people turned and stared.

Regaining their composure, Marta fished a tissue out of her suit jacket pocket and handed it to Emily to wipe away the joyous tears streaming down her freckles. "Well, what now, Luv?" said Marta.

"I'll find us a place while Alessio is in Boston, and maybe by the time Jason surfaces, I'll be out of the condo. So, what's up with the loony toon?"

"I watched him on TV Sunday morning. Don't suppose you happened to catch it?"

Sunday morning, she had been lying next to Alessio, the two of them listening to Andreas

Vollenweider music on the public radio station, happily arguing about whether Vollenweider was pop music or semi-classical. The good-natured wrangling came to an abrupt halt when Alessio rolled over on her, pinned her to the bed, and started kissing her, starting with her eyelids and working his way toe-ward.

"No. I was busy."

"Yeah, well, this guy, Angler, has got balls. He stood there, in his designer suit, with his dyed toupee looking totally freaky on top of that old, square face, with his capped teeth and manicured nails, and he told his congregation God had given him the power to cure cancer, so they had to send money so he could reach out and save people from this terrible disease! Do you believe it? Then he told them the reason they were sick is because they were living in sin, so come to Water's Edge, stay in our hotel, bring all your money to pay for our counseling, and we will make you well."

"Isn't that against the law?" said Emily.

"Nope. It's freedom of religion in America."

"Well, trying to set up a judge with a prostitute is against the law, isn't it?" Emily said.

"Only if it's for the purpose of blackmailing him later, which we cannot prove unless someone is willing to testify," said Marta. "We know they tried the same thing with a judge in Oklahoma, but nobody could ever prove it."

"Got time to walk?"

Marta didn't answer, just stood up and stretched high with her arms and bent from side to side a few times.

"Now I'm ready," she said.

Instead of cutting across the grass, Emily and Marta stayed on the walkway leading to the water's edge. While walking, Emily silently recalled the Oklahoma case.

An extortion plot by the Chrions to compromise a U.S. magistrate presiding over a child abuse trial resulted in an attempt to lure the judge into a compromising position involving an eleven-year-old girl.

The state was claiming the Chrions mentally and physically abused children of parents belonging to the sect.

At first, the judge had taken the traditional position regarding parents' rights to raise their children as they saw fit. But when he began to suspect the state might have a case, the Chrions attacked him. They planted spies in the courthouse and bugged his telephone, then began spreading rumors that he had a thing for little girls. In a state of exhaustion and near-collapse, the judge withdrew from the case and eventually was hospitalized with a stroke.

"What are you thinking about?" Marta said, expecting to hear Emily answer "Alessio, of course."

Instead, Emily said, "What happened to that case in Oklahoma?"

"Thrown out on a technicality," Marta said. "So what else is new."

"So that left them free to carry on . . ."

". . . in the name of Jesus!" Marta completed Emily's thought.

"Speaking of Jesus, what do you want for Christmas?"

"A clone of Alessio."

EIGHT—EMILY TELLS JASON

Monday evening Emily arranged to meet a real estate agent on Tuesday morning, just north of Water's Edge, in Brystal Beach, a hidden-away community of dwellers who minded their own business and did not ask questions about their neighbors. Some lived in shanties while others lived in waterfront mansions.

Emily went home to begin packing. She wanted to be out of the house by the time Jason returned. She still did not know where he was. Another 24 hours and she would have to put out a missing persons.

She expected to feel at least a little melancholy over leaving, but she didn't. She gathered her clothes into suitcases, packed her shoes and boots into boxes, and placed her jewel case, containing only two pairs of earrings, inside her makeup bag, which was filled with potions she rarely applied, other than mascara on her lashes. Before tackling the books, she sat down to rest in the den.

Watching through the window, she could see the ninth tee. Despite the fact that it was hot again, fifteen degrees warmer than yesterday, neighbors were out for their afternoon round, wearing color-coordinated Innisbrook shirts, Sawgrass caps, and Beene trousers.

Cocooned inside, Emily noticed the air conditioning had not shut off even though it was set on eighty-two degrees, and the ceiling fans were running. Golfers are crazy, she said to the furniture. I'd be hauled away by the medics after an hour in this heat.

Emily watched, as out on the ninth tee Henry Walker raised the leather flask to his lips before slicing one to the left. Mary Walker paused to sip daintily from silver before she hooked one to the right. Do they have to drink to stand each other?

Frowning, the Walkers both climbed back into their cart, drove one hundred feet down the fairway and got back out of the cart. They cut a V, him looking for his lost left slice, her seeking the right hook. My, they seemed to be having fun Emily told the lamps. At least they are trying. Maybe after enough sipping, slicing, and hooking they feel like making out in a sand trap. No, not a sand trap. Mary would hate sand in her hair. Did she always? I didn't.

Sand in my hair and under my fingernails.

Emily replayed in her mind the scene of Alessio and her, silently leaving their room and making their way down the beach to the place where artificial sand dunes provided cover from prying eyes. It was dark, the moon had set, stars twinkled in an indigo sky, the welcome weight of his body, crushing, crushing, crushing. His mouth, his lips, his tongue, giving life, life, life, *oh please, don't let this end.*

She picked up her pink journal and started to pack it. Where is the blue one?

"Emily," Jason shouted from the front door.

"In here," she answered. "I was concerned."

"I'm sorry. I was visiting mother and her phone was out."

Jason looked around at the mess of boxes. Emily watched his face pale even more than usual. He seemed stultified. She did not want this. This was not his fault.

"Are you leaving me?"

"Do you mind terribly?"

"Yes, of course. But I understand it."

"You do?"

"Yes, you've been seen meeting a man for lunch several times lately.

Seen?

"I'm sorry, Jason. Yes, it is true."

"You're leaving me for him?"

"Yes."

"I see."

I see. Just those words. I see.

Tuesday morning Emily signed a one-year lease on a well-furnished house, tucked away in an inlet overlooking St. James Sound. Islands too small for habitation provided shelter for seabirds and small sailboats when the sudden storms made the intercoastal waterway impassable.

Alessio would have a home to come to when he returned from Boston, where he had gone to collect his things and resign from the *Boston Times*. One quick phone call to the *Tampa Chronicle* had assured him of a position whenever he wanted it. Emily's paper was not big enough to support a full-time music critic, and besides, it would appear uncouth—not to mention tacky—for Alessio to be working for a newspaper that Jason partly owned.

NINE—SCANDALS

Emily could not believe what she was seeing. A newsletter put out by the Chrions, stating that Marta had an illegitimate child and Emily and Alessio are living in sin.

"Alessio and I are no secret, but where did they get this about Marta? Hospital records are supposed to be private," she said.

"They are out of control," said Eddy. "Is it true?"

"Well, yes. She gave birth to a baby sixteen years ago—stillborn they said. They told Marta the child had been accidentally cremated before Marta ever got a chance to see it. But they said it was a little girl."

"They have made their tactics well known," said Eddy, shoving a report across her desk, written by Sal, the reporter Eddy sent in undercover.

Emily picked up the report and started reading:

The discovery in Water's Edge that

documents were missing from the District Attorney's office suggests that in this field, Christionologists are experts. Denigrating articles continue to be generated on a regular basis and published in their newsletter, The Christionologist.

Archibald T. Angler, claiming his authority comes from God, has instigated the gathering of intelligence by methods far more sophisticated than his experience would suggest. Whatever the source of his information, there is no doubt that Archibald T. Angler well understands the principles of espionage.

"The defense of our religion is unnecessary. This is America. God is on our side."

The clatter of IBM Selectrics manned by harried reporters on deadline churning out blocks of copy designed to fit that day's news hole disrupted Emily's concentration. Saturdays in the newsroom were especially noisy, even though the paper was laid out except for Section A.

Copy editors running up and down the stairs, checking layouts and making corrections concerned themselves with nothing else but not being chewed out by Eddy on Monday morning for overlooking a dumb typo. All typos were dumb to Eddy.

Emily's column ran this morning, so the bit in the newsletter about her and Alessio living in sin apparently was printed before her column appeared. She was thankful Jason had stopped coming to the paper. They had always worked in separate buildings, the administrative side being separated from the editorial side. Now, Emily was glad she did not have to face him, and as for what people were thinking, she just did not care. She was content in Alessio's company every night, re-energizing herself to support Marta's growing determination to stop the Christionologists no matter what it took. Now she will really be out to get them.

The newsroom grew frantic as the deadline for the Sunday paper approached, the wire clicked and clattered, bringing stories from other papers, for consideration for publication in the *Water's Edge Daily News.*

Emily's phone rang. It was Alessio, calling from the *Tampa Chronicle.*

"A story is coming over the wire from this morning's paper. Get it and read it yourself," he said.

The tone of his voice alarmed Emily. She hurried over to the wire desk and waited for the paper to unroll out of the machine.

May 26, 1979

TAMPA—Jason Wohl, owner of the *Water's Edge Daily News,* was arrested Friday night after residents living along the section of Dale Mabry Highway known as the Dale Mabry Gayway took the law into their own hands, claiming to be disgusted with police efforts to clean up their neighborhood.

Carrying sledgehammers, torches and signs reading, 'If you're gay, stay away,' seven men and two women smashed in doors at the Palms of Paradise Motel, in the 4600 block, and set fire to mattresses while surprised occupants fled for their lives.

Wohl, 42, and an unidentified man were forced by smoke to leave the room they occupied. Police, who arrived on the scene shortly after being called by the motel's owner Pat Jericho, arrested Wohl, apparently unable to retrieve his clothes, for public nudity. The unidentified man drove away in a yellow Cadillac, witnesses said, carrying his clothes and wearing only a motel towel and black socks."

Emily scanned the rest of the story, enough to determine Jason had been booked and released, then took the story into Eddy, who read it while he chewed on a pencil. By the time he finished, he had so many little wood chips in his mustache he resembled a walrus.

"Geez, Emily, I'm sorry," Eddy said. "I never expected this! What do you want me to do?"

"You knew?"

"You didn't? Geez, I thought that's why you left him."

Eddy dropped his eyes, but Emily saw the love in them.

"I'm sorry, Em."

"Treat it like you would anything else that happens in Tampa," Emily said, knowing that meant one graf on the state page.

"The cop reporter who got this must be new," said Eddy. "Otherwise they'd be knocking down our doors."

"If other papers call, I'm not available for comment. They will have a field day with this and crucify Jason all by themselves. They don't need me to help them."

Emily did not miss and was grateful for the irony of Jason's timing. A Saturday paper, heavy news, a small news hole. Jason's copy had to compete with John Spenkelink's electrocution on May 25th, the day before, in Tallahassee, the first person executed in the U.S. in two years. On top of that, 272 people aboard an American Airlines DC 10, plus three men on the ground, were killed on the same day after the plane lost one of its engines and crashed shortly after takeoff from Chicago's O'Hare International Airport. Two of the passengers were from Tampa. That meant reporters from the *Chronicle,* and all three TV stations were tripping all over each other to interview the grieving families. If it bleeds, it leads. Only Jason's soul was bleeding. By the time they finished with Spenkelink and the air disaster, Jason would be old news. They would leave him alone until someone remembered there was a juicy scandal shaping up over in Water's Edge.

TEN—MARTA, HAM, AND MANDINO

Marta Miller squinted her eyes in the direction of the clock, but couldn't make out the time or the date, 26 May 1979.

"The rest of me is only 38, but my eyes are 88," she said aloud to Clone, the cat.

Ham, the slam-bam-thank-you-ma'am lover, was sleeping in his apartment for a change. One more slip up, and he was out of there. Permanently. Marta had enough troubles without Ham thinking he could come and go at will. What she needed was a real lover that could make her forget everything. Then maybe she wouldn't drink so much.

Fat chance.

Marta envied Emily her Alessio. The magnificent Alessio.

Just whom am I kidding? I don't know another man

who even comes close.

Naked, she slopped her way to the kitchen to pour the coffee, ready through the miracle of self-starting coffee makers. She trekked back to the bedroom for a robe and slippers and tripped over the cat.

"Move the hell out of the way, Clone."

Clone scampered out the door ahead of Marta bending down to pick up the *Daily News* from the hallway.

He'd hover around the outside door until someone came along to let him out. He knew the routine.

Clone was chocolate brown with gray eyes that matched the worn bells on his black leather collar. He was company when Ham wasn't around.

Shoving yesterday's mail out of the way, she thought about the phone call she received just as she was leaving the office. The girl said her name was Holly. She had seen Marta on television asking for information about who was stealing babies, mutilating them, then discarding them in trash cans. Marta spread the newspaper out on the counter, half dreading what she might find. Another editorial about the Christionologists this morning.

Keep 'em coming, Emily. That's my girl.

Marta had always felt protective toward Emily. Treated her more like a daughter than a friend, even though they were the same age.

Are the Christionologists winning?
by Emily Mason

The organization calling themselves a religion, but who are better known as the cult, Christionology, had big plans for this unsuspecting community when it arrived here two years ago. In essence, the sect wanted to control the city's politicians, media, and religious groups. They looked at how most of us are from someplace else, our lack of cohesiveness, and we must have looked like easy pickings.

To that end, the Chrions apparently have succeeded. Hardly any Water's Edge resident is even aware of the sect's secret goals and reform activities. Nevertheless, the group has purchased $10 million in Water's Edge property and continues to work for the potential to exert the political pressure it needs to gain acceptance.

Documents released by the FBI, as well as activities of the Chrions in Water's Edge, indicate the sect has no intention of letting up in its quest to take over the city.

Are we going to sit by? This would be mind your own business gone wrong.

Marta began scanning the document,

upon which the editorial was based, and upon which Clone liked to lay atop Marta's kitchen counter:

In December 1975, top "church" leaders, slipped into Water's Edge under the false name of Christian Brotherhood, with the stated purpose of making allies of religious and local government opinion leaders, according to the documents. The next step, Chrion correspondence shows, was to attempt to discredit groups or persons who did not support the Christian Brotherhood.

"If we face opposition, we must, by any and all means, destroy our enemies."

Clandestine infiltration into local media and other organizations was the prerequisite for achieving their objectives. To that end, they began secretly placing members in local businesses, for the expressed purpose of keeping tabs on dissenting voices against their presence.

Christionologists apparently believe they must be ever vigilant against any threat that could succeed in weakening their position in Water's Edge.

"It is from this place that we shall spread our message to the planet, and we will unite the world order into one religion known as Christionology."

The world order into one religion. Mmmm, I don't think so. Not unless I get to pick it.

Marta heard Clone's collar jingle at the front door.

"No luck, huh, boy?" she said, opening the door, where stood Ham, holding out Clone like a quart of milk.

"I believe you lost this?" Ham said, walking through the doorway without waiting to be asked in.

"Why so early, Ham?" said Marta, taking Clone and dropping him onto the sofa that matched his chocolate brown fur. Easier on the furniture to match the cat than the other way around.

She wasn't ready to tell Ham about the phone call from Holly.

"Lovely," said Ham. "Come get in the shower and let me give you a rubdown before you dress for work. You look like you could use it."

"It's Saturday."

"You're not going in to work?"

"I didn't say that."

Marta decided he was right and let him lead her

into the bathroom. She took off her robe and turned on the water while Ham removed his tan suit, light blue shirt, and dark blue tie and laid them out carefully so as not to wrinkle before he put them back on.

She waited patiently for him under the steamy hot water. He finally got through fussing with his clothes and stepped into the tub alongside her. She allowed herself to relax into his hands, those skillful hands. She'd once said to Emily, "It is too bad the rest of him doesn't work as well as his hands."

He lathered her back and gently pressed his thumbs into her shoulder blades, sending the tension in her shoulders down the drain with the bubbles. She raised her arms above her head, spread her legs as she had done a thousand times before, and let Ham and the soap do their work.

He washed her and rinsed her, then turned off the water and there in the shower tongued her dry. He knew that always made her feel as though she needed another bath, so he turned the water back on and rinsed her all over again. Then he led her to the bed and dried her with a towel before he entered. Marta counted down, silently: ten, nine, eight, seven, six, five, four, three, two, one. Blast off.

Marta's mind flicked open, and Erich Mandino floated by.

Bad timing, Marta. Very uncouth. One man at a time.
"Wow, what a woman. I love you, Marta."

"I love you, too, Ham."

And she did. She just wished he lasted longer.

Ham slipped back into his neatly arranged clothes and headed for the kitchen to make breakfast. Marta dressed and ate Ham's frozen waffles even though she didn't want them. She ate them because she always ate them, just like she always let him fuck her. Why not? To Marta's way of thinking, you gotta eat, and you gotta get laid. On the way out the door, she found herself thinking, *I'm in a rut.*

"*Goodamighty.* Would you look at this traffic," she said to the air, switching on the car radio, hoping to hear a traffic report that would steer her around this jam. Instead the news was on:

On the local scene, a baby's body has been found in a trashcan outside Water's Edge Hospital, mutilated in a similar fashion to the body of the baby found last week in Sawgrass County. Police offer no clues as to the identity of the lunatic responsible for these deaths. The stock market this week . . . .

Marta switched off the radio. She felt like she'd upchuck Ham's waffles. Instead, she placed her portable red light on top of her car and turned on her siren, but it did no good. The traffic had no place to go. Finally, she just drove up onto the sidewalk past the jam-up and hollered at the officers working the accident up ahead.

"Get this mess cleared up, Rookie."

The young officer recognized her and shouted, "Wait, Miss Miller. You'll be interested in this."

Marta wheeled her car around sideways in the street, got out, and rushed over to the smashed blue sedan with the Sawgrass County license plates. There in the back floorboard of the car lay a newborn baby, dead from the impact of the crash, its tiny body wrapped in a Water's Edge Hospital sheet. The driver of the car, an elderly man with a strawberry scar on his head, was dead. He wore a tiny golden fox on a small chain around his neck.

Marta, numb, said, "Sorry about the 'rookie' crack, Officer. Tell Detective Mandino I'll be in touch."

Later in Marta's office, she told him about receiving a phone call from a young prostitute who said she wanted to help find out who is going around killing babies.

Mandino was furious. "What else do you know, Miller, that you're not telling?"

"Don't get your bump in a hump," said Marta. "I'm not holding out. I only talked to this girl yesterday. I didn't tell you because there was nothing to tell. Yet."

"Yet? What do you mean, yet? What do you expect to find out?"

"Maybe nothing. Maybe a lot. But I don't want your sloths dogging her tail, maybe getting her killed before she has a chance to lead us to the killer."

"Really, Miller. This is withholding evidence. I should throw your butt in jail."

"Who's gonna charge me? Me? And then what?"

Mandino was so frustrated all he could do was sputter.

"And then . . .and then . . . ."

"You're a joke, Mandino. Your blue boys will mess up the search, and a bleeding heart judge will throw out the case on a friggin' technicality. We're talking child killers here, Mandino. Sex crimes. They're murdering babies. And you're screaming at me for not telling you about a hooker who might lead us to the killers? You're a joke."

Marta noticed the vein pulsing in his right temple.

"Now you listen to me, Miller. I'm taking this bull from you only because I want these monsters as badly as you do. And I don't give a rip if we never get this one into court. If I find the mothers first, I'll blow 'em away myself."

"Ok, Duke, now you're talking. Maybe you aren't all bad."

"But listen, Miller, you can't play this one by yourself. It's too dangerous. You let me in on what you know."

"You'll play it my way?

"Hell, Woman."

"My way or not at all."

"Dammit all, you hard-headed, obstinate female. You'll get yourself killed and me thrown off the force."

"My way."

"Maybe."

"Not good enough."

"I said Maybe!"

"And I said that's not good enough. I'm calling the shots here, Mandino, and if you don't like it, there's the door!"

Mandino whirled around and headed out. Suddenly, he stopped and turned to face Marta.

"Okay." His voice was quiet.

"Okay, what?"

"We'll do it your way."

Marta smiled and noticed he was good-looking when he wasn't yelling.

"Tell me about the girl," he said.

"Later. I have to meet Emily. Jason's been arrested.

"Aren't they divorced?"

"Separated—six months thereabouts."

"What's the charge?"

"Public nudity. Indecent exposure. Something like that."

"Where?"

"Tampa."

"Bet you're glad of that."

"It would be awkward if I had to prosecute."

"Get back to me on the girl."

"Will do."

Emily was waiting for her on their bench. She had called immediately about Jason's arrest, but Marta was so distraught over the dead baby she had not told her about the newsletter.

"Let's walk," said Marta.

Emily handed her the newsletter.

Marta looked at it for a long minute, then said, "Well, ain't this some fine sack of sunflower seeds.

m sorry, Em. I know this was hard for you showing me this."

"Let's get 'em."

"You betcha," said Marta.

They hugged each other.

"I read the police reports. Have you called Holly to set up a meeting?" Emily said.

"No. I'm waiting to see if someone else will come forward to identify the man with the strawberry scar. I don't want to waste Holly on this when she might lead us to Angler. Tomorrow or the next day will be soon enough. I left orders to guard that infant's body and not burn it."

"Are you okay?" Emily asked.

"Sure. Detective Mandino's on my back about

withholding evidence. What do you think of him?"

"Good looking. Sensitive. Sweet."

"Are we talking about the same Erich Jasper Mandino?" said Marta.

"Jasper?"

"Yeah. I pulled his files. That's his middle name. Jasper."

"I bet you could start a fight if you called him that."

"It takes less, believe me. I'm thinking of trusting him. Should I?"

"With what?"

"Holly, of course. What did you think I meant?"

"How's Ham?"

"Fast. As always. Why did you bring him up?"

"No reason. Do you think Mandino can help?"

"With what?" Marta said.

"Holly, of course. What did you think I meant?"

"I think I have to let him try. Another baby this morning. That makes three. It can't go on."

"Tomorrow's editorial will be rough," Emily warned. "Eddy is enjoying that I turned over the Sunday editorials to him."

"Can't you hold him off? When he starts pontificating about police inefficiency, he just gets things more riled up."

"Eddy doesn't listen to me. Besides, writing editorials about tragedies makes his day. He hates it when things are calm."

"He has nice teeth."

"Who"

"Erich. You know I like nice teeth."

"So do I," Emily said.

ELEVEN—HOLLY

Thursday evening, Emily arrived at Jack's around 7:30 and slid into the smoky booth where Marta sat, drinking vodka. Emily studied her face for signs that she'd had too much to make sense. But her clear, green eyes glowed brightly with hope.

"Have a sit and drink," she said. "Holly's on her way."

Emily obeyed and waited for Marta to say more. Jack, the bartender, brought over single malt Islay for Emily, but Marta waited for him to get out of earshot before she spoke again.

"This sixteen-year-old hooker walking in here any minute may be the key," Marta said.

"How?"

"She says she knows Angler intimately if you

know what I mean," said Marta, her face drawn with disgust at the thought of that vile little toad with a teenager.

"She's willing to help because of the dead babies. And Emily, she was and still is one of the Christionologists."

"Here she comes."

Marta slid over to make room.

Emily watched Marta greet this whore child as though she were a long-lost daughter. Her warmth seemed unusual to Emily, who knew her friend to be exceedingly cautious with strangers, even young ones.

Holly slid into the booth next to Marta and turned her blue-eyed innocent gaze onto Emily

Emily thought were it not for the spiky blond mane and the gaudy junk hanging around her neck, she would bear an uncanny resemblance to Marta.

Emily spotted one small trinket among her necklaces that may not have been junk. A golden animal hanging from a silk thread. A closer look showed it to be a tiny fox.

"Do you have a last name, Holly?" said Emily.

"Just call me Holly, please," she said, not offering to shake hands with Emily, but keeping her hands folded in her lap.

Emily chuckled, wondering if she had expected Holly to greet her as though she was bucking for a corporate vice presidency.

"I'll call you Holly if you call me Emily," she said, and then fell silent. This was Marta's show.

"Holly, Emily is a reporter. She's been investigating the murders. She is also my friend and your friend. You can tell her anything," Marta said, hoping to help Holly relax.

Emily did not turn on the tape recorder in her purse, fearful Holly would freeze up. Emily did not want to frighten her for any reason. If this girl talked, it could break this case.

"I . . . I just don't want you to think I had anything to do with what's been happening to the babies. I didn't even know about it. It wasn't like that with us," said Holly.

"Where do you live, Holly?" Marta said.

"Now I live at the Sanctuary, that big old hotel place, downtown. But I was at the farm all my life."

"The farm?" said Marta.

"All my life," Holly said. "It was the only home I ever knew. We were treated good, except for what they made us do. They fed us and kept us warm."

"Who are they, Holly?" Marta said, "and how many are there?"

"The Keepers," she said. "Mostly old women and a few old men when we were real little. They loved us and looked after us. The Trainers were younger. They trained us what to do and how to act. They never hurt us or nothing That's why I can't figure who's killing the babies."

Marta shuddered, visible the anger inside her. She downed her Vodka and ordered another.

"Would you care for anything, Holly?" Emily said.

"Yes, ma'am, I don't drink, but I'll have a soda if that's okay."

"Me too," said Emily. "No more booze tonight."

In the low lighting, Emily could not be sure, but Holly's eye color seemed to be the same as Marta's, blue with a greenish tinge that changed with the colors she wore. Holly's hands were clean, but like Marta's, her fingernails were chewed. Holly was wearing a strapless striped knit top, and Emily could see her well-outlined, beautiful clavicles, which happened to be one of Marta's best features. Jack brought over the drinks and left them alone.

"Do you know who your parents were?" Marta said.

"No ma'am. I've never known anything but the farm, until now. But I've been thinking and wondering if I might have been kidnapped from a hospital like these other babies, only I didn't end up dead, I mean... here I am and all...maybe the Snatchers...."

"Whoa . . . hold on, little girl. What about school?"

"They teach us on the farm. That's what I heard them called, the Snatchers. Granny K would say, 'I'll be busy today, Holly. The Snatchers are coming in.' I didn't know it meant anything bad until lately. Every week or so new babies would be brought to the farm in West Sawgrass."

"Geezus," Marta glared at Emily.

"Go on, Holly," Emily said.

"New babies would be brought in cryin' and hollerin' for their mamas, and The Keepers would rock them and settle them down. There was even a doctor who'd come check'em over," Holly said.

Marta's jaw dropped.

"Emily, it's just like we figured. A doctor is involved."

"I have the feeling we have heard nothing yet," Emily said.

"We were given everything," said Holly. "Spoiled, I guess you'd say. Like one time I remember I wouldn't perform. That's what it was called, performing. Anyway, Granny K, she was sort of like my nanny, was real upset because all of a sudden I didn't want to do it anymore. I guess I was about eight, and I didn't like the smell of it. I just sat down and said, 'No.' Granny K brought me a pill and a new doll that talked to me. I don't know how they did it, but the doll told me how sad Angel would be if I didn't perform. I still didn't want to do it, but the doll talked me into it."

"*What angel?*" Marta demanded. This was the first time they were hearing of any "angel."

"Easy, there. We don't want to scare Holly," said Emily.

"Angel is all I know," said Holly, "who would be sad if we didn't perform. I never saw . . . come to think of it, I don't know if Angel is a man or a woman angel. But I don't know how things went from an Angel to dead babies. Something must have gone wrong."

"Where do they get the babies?" Emily said.

"From all over, I guess. See, I kinda think the hospitals tell the mamas the babies was born dead. That way nobody comes looking for 'em. Then they sell 'em to the Snatchers."

Marta asked her if she had any idea who would want to hurt the babies.

"Only Angel says what gets done. The reason I say that is that Granny K didn't want me to be put out on the street. She tried to fix it so I could become a Trainer and not have to leave the farm. But Angel said no . . . that I'd make more people happy in service on the street," Holly said, fingering the tiny golden fox. "So Granny K packed my stuff. She was crying when I left. Goobey drove me here to Water's Edge and put me up in the Sanctuary. That's where I live now. It's a real nice place, but like I said, something's gone wrong."

Marta and Emily looked at each other, reading one another's disbelief that anyone could be as naive and innocent as Holly seemed to be. Apparently, she had been drugged and hypnotized, and in a way sheltered from reality all of her life.

"This Goobey," said Marta, "what else does he do at the farm beside drive girls to the Sanctuary?"

"Goobey takes care of the animals. He really likes the sheep. They like him, too," answered Holly.

"I'll just bet . . ." Marta said.

"Do you trust Granny K and Goobey?" said Emily.

"I trust everybody, or I used to. I know Angel is the only one who gives orders, and, now, with the babies and all . . . I think things aren't like they used to be."

"Is there any way you can find out who Angel is? Does anybody know for sure? Who talks to him?" Emily said.

Emily was presuming Angel was a man. What woman would mutilate a baby boy and leave him to bleed to death?

The way Marta slugged down that last vodka, she must have been thinking the same thought. Except, Emily hadn't seen the bodies. Marta had.

"What made you phone Marta?" Emily said.

"I saw her on TV talking about the babies. She looked so sad, and I wanted to help her," Holly answered, looking toward Marta as though she wanted to hug her. Instead, she reached over and patted Marta's arm.

Marta started to draw back, and then she

relaxed, realizing Holly meant kindness. Touching was as natural as breathing to Holly. The Trainers had seen to that.

"Aren't you afraid of what Angel will do if he knows you're helping us?" Marta asked Holly.

"I guess so, but I guess I'm more afraid of what will happen if I don't help," Holly answered.

"Do you know the Reverend Archibald T. Angler?" said Emily.

Marta and Emily looked at each other in silent agreement that he might be Angel, but neither was prepared for what Holly would say.

"Oh, sure, I know him. He comes to the Sanctuary a lot. More lately than before. And he prays more now than he did. I think something is bothering him."

"Does he talk to you?" said Marta.

"Not really. He just makes me lie on a table and spread my legs. He kneels down there and prays into my . . . you know. He cries sometimes and prays out loud about entering the 'throne of Grace.' Then he calls me Grace. Sometimes he acts like he's trying to crawl inside me and be born again. He talks a lot about being born again. He says things like, 'No man shall be saved unless he enters at the throne of Grace and is born again.' I think he's talking to himself, not to me. My name's not Grace. He's a little nutso if you ask me. But harmless enough, I guess. I mean, he's never said anything to make me think he'd hurt anybody."

This had to be the dumbest girl Emily and Marta had ever seen.

"There's just one thing," Holly went on. "Most of the time I don't really listen to what he's saying, 'cause, like I said, he's mostly talking to hisself. But last time he said some different things. He was sayin' stuff like, 'male and female created he them,' and 'Thou shalt not spill thy seed upon the ground.' Things like that. Then he sort of chanted over and over, 'the blood, the blood, the saving blood.' Right afterwards was when I heard about what happened to that baby boy. It seemed to me that somebody was trying the make a little boy into a girl, sort of like 'male and female' . . . ."

Maybe Holly wasn't so dumb after all.

"When will you see him again?" said Emily.

"I never know when he's coming Oh! That reminds me. When he comes, you know, climaxes, he never does it inside of me. He screams, 'Defile not the temple,' and lets it fly into the air. Then he yells, the rapture! the rapture! and falls on the floor and makes me sit on his face. I've never seen a man so obsessed with eatin' . . . you know . . . down there . . . as he is. It's like he's trying to turn hisself into one."

Marta said to Emily, "Maybe we should bug her room."

"Are you sure you want to listen to that?"

"Cunnilingus is illegal in this state. We could arrest him for statutory rape."

"You want to bring him in on weird sex charges?" Emily said.

"Of course not. I want to execute the bastard for murder," Marta said.

Holly interrupted. "You really think he's the Angel?"

"Will you help us find out?" said Marta.

Little Holly, in one way dumb as a door, in another way resourceful as hell—she'd stayed alive, hadn't she—said, "Sure, I'll help."

Leaving Jack's, Emily tried to snuff out the sound of Holly's innocent voice with the Jaguar's motor. Holly had disappeared into the misty night after refusing a ride back to the Sanctuary.

Goobey trailed a few feet behind her and watched to see no harm came to her. Holly shouldn't be seen riding in a reporter's car. *They wouldn't like it.*

Marta took a cab. She'd had too much to drink to drive.

Alessio was waiting up for Emily when she arrived at the house they had rented about six months ago. He stood a foot taller and outweighed Emily by one hundred pounds. But his gentleness matched his beauty. He lifted her sweetly and carried her to the bedroom, where, for once, his lovemaking did not include oral sex, for which she was grateful this night. Emily would be awhile shaking the images planted by Holly of Angler worshipping at the throne of Grace.

The next morning Alessio made coffee while Emily dug through her notes and filled him in on Holly's story, leaving out some of the sex part. She especially needed to read what she had found about an ancient cult suspected of child pornography, kidnapping, and Satan worship. Emily wondered how Holly had come out of that, innocent and even eager to help. Granny K must be somehow different. And Goobey had not sounded evil. Just kinky. The animal rights people would be interested. But later. Not now. Protecting sheep is the least of it with babies being murdered.

Alessio poured steaming black coffee into yellow mugs and sat his white terry-wrapped frame down on the barstool across from Emily. Sunlight streaming into the breakfast room lit his shiny dark hair. Being with Alessio made it all bearable for Emily. She read through her notes, then called Marta, bracing herself for Marta's *WHAT?* Which was the way she answered the phone when awakened, especially if she had a hangover, which Emily suspected she must have.

"*What!* yourself. Wake up and get out your

Bible. Read up on the archangel, as in Archibald T. It would be just like this loony toon to name himself something like that, especially if he thinks he can be born again by crawling into Holly."

Alessio looked up, sorry he'd missed the conversation the night before.

"What's the plan with Holly?" Emily said.

"She's calling when he shows up again."

TWELVE—GRANNY K

Holly opened her eyes wondering if last night had been a dream. She dreamed often. Sometimes dreaming was her favorite thing to do. It was better than watching television because dreams don't have commercials and better than reading because the Guardian in the dream explains the story as it goes along. The Guardian explains things even better than Granny K.

Last night wasn't a dream. She actually talked to Marta Miller, the lady she saw on TV. She and Miz Wohl were nice. Almost nice as Granny K.

Nobody could be like Granny K. She's special. So gentle, so kind, yet so protective she keeps an Uzi under her chair.

Holly could not tell if Granny K meant it when she had hugged her and called her a little soothsayer.

"Precious child, you are extraordinary. The world must never touch you."

THIRTEEN—JASON'S SHAME

A couple of weeks later after his arrest Emily received a call from Jason. No one knew where he had been hiding since being arrested.

"Please, Emily. Come to the house," he begged, sounding so pitiful Emily almost felt compassion for him.

She also figured he wanted to discuss the divorce. He had surprised her by saying he was signing the newspaper over to her, and she thought this would be their last meeting. Their lawyers could take it from here.

Emily was not prepared for Jason's shame over his arrest. When she arrived, it was dark. She cursed that elusive keyhole, wondering why Jason had not turned on the outside lights. His black Cadillac in the driveway let her know he was inside, waiting.

Once inside the foyer, she could see him slumped on the sofa in front of a soundless TV. "Jason," she said, her tingling skin warning that his slack-jawed face and mixmaster hair, usually so neatly combed, heralded showdown.

By the light of the TV, she could see his shoulders drooping and his arms loosely dangling. Then, at the sound of her footsteps, his fist clenched, and he winced in pain.

"Your hands…"

She started to ask about the bandages on his hands, but the voice that spoke chilled her.

"It's all over, Emily," he said.

"Have you been drinking? What did you do to your hands?"

"What the hell difference does it make?"

He whimpered. Raised his head. Emily flipped on a light to a face raw with pain. Jason's mask was off.

Wide-opened pupils. His eyes resembled black holes in a skull.

Emily winced but forced herself to look at him. Cold, gut fear gripped her as the holes in his skeleton eyes burned into her brain the image of her own broken, dying body slipping off jagged rocks into the water. She felt herself watching from high on a cliff, as the waves below swallowed the hem of a bloody dress. At high tide, she'd be washed out to sea. In her mind, ocher teeth behind the leer began to elongate and the face transformed into the dogface jackal in my dream.

I'm going to die again, only this time, Jason is going to

kill me himself.

He seemed still enough, there on the sofa, but his clenched fist revealed his rage. Then suddenly, pulling his defenses around him, like a lie warding off a chilling truth, Jason stood up.

Emily's fear deflated into disgust.

Oh God he's going to be reasonable. His resources are drying up before my eyes, and soon there will be nothing left but dust where he stands.

She took her bag off her shoulder and laid it on the teak dining room table.

Jason uncharacteristically hitched up his britches, stepped over to the table now between them, and leaned forward. He steadied himself by placing his palms down on the table, clearly revealing the bloody cuts on his knuckles the bandages didn't cover.

The light overhead wobbled slightly as the fan whirled, sending flickers down the walls, making the room feel more alive than Jason. His grayish brown eyes, merely beady and a little bloodshot most times were now rimmed sorely red, from drinking and crying. Red rims around black holes in a skull. His nose, usually straight and fine, was puffy and bulbous. Skeleton eyes and a P.T. Barnum nose. Always handsome in a fragile sort of way, now he seemed ugly. His light brown messy hair looked greasy, and he was so tense he might shatter.

Then, his slender body sank into itself, and he

reached out with one well-manicured finger and delicately touched one of the white silk flowers that made up the arrangement in the center of the table. He appeared ragged and bloated, but calm, too calm. He kept his head down, never once looking at Emily.

Interminable moments passed.

It's like watching hatred metastasize. Does he hate himself or me?

Then, without warning, Jason clutched his face with his hands. He started screaming, partly in pain, partly in mental anguish, "I can't look at you, Emily. I'd rather die than look at you."

He gouged his fingers deeply into black holes in his skull. Blood gushed from his skeleton eye sockets, spurting across the table, the flowers, the purse, Emily.

Horrified and too stunned to scream, Emily rushed to the kitchen phone and dialed 911, struggled to keep her composure as Jason screamed in the background, "Kill me, Emily, kill me, Emily. Don't make me face it. I have to die. I have to die."

He passed out quickly from the pain. Emily harnessed enough common sense to give the address to the 911 operator. Then she called Marta.

"I'm at the house with Jason. He . . . He's . . . just come. Can you come? You have to come. The blood . . . just come."

"On my way. Do I need to call anyone? Are you

all right?"

"I called 911. Just come."

"Hang up. I'm on my way."

Emily obeyed Marta and put the phone back in its cradle on the wall. A bloody thumbprint on the receiver made her look at my hands.

Blood on my hands. My clothes. Jason's blood. Oh God, Jason.

She grabbed a towel off the counter and ran back into the dining room to kneel beside Jason to try to stop the blood. But the sight of him, crumpled, drawn into the fetal position, blood oozing from the right eye socket, obscuring what appeared to be the eyeball, lying on the bridge of his nose, sent her reeling backwards, gagging in horror.

She could not go near him. Only stand in the doorway, arms wrapped around herself, rocking backward and forward, stomach churning, mind absent until the sound of the doorbell jarred her back into herself.

The paramedics came inside and took Jason to Water's Edge Hospital just as Marta was arriving. She beat the police there.

Marta ignored the blood on Emily's clothes and hugged her close.

"Tell me," she said.

"I couldn't go to the hospital with him. I guess I should have, but all this..." She disengaged herself from Marta's arms and stepped back, looking down at the blood.

"Look at . . . me."

"You're in shock, Luv."

"Oh, Marta, he . . . his eye . . . he . . . took his hands and.." She put her hands up to her eyes, attempting to demonstrate what Jason did.

"One of his eyeballs was just lying there, all bloody."

She couldn't stop sobbing.

"The police will here in a minute. Try to pull yourself together. Have you called Alessio?"

"Oh, no, Alessio! No, no, I haven't called him," she said, pushing back away from Marta.

"I don't feel like Jason's wife anymore. I feel more than estranged, I feel detached, as though Jason were someone I once knew but not anymore."

Marta picked the blood-spattered purse up off the dining room table and handed it to Emily. She slipped the strap over her shoulder. We both knew better than to touch anything until the police finished their reports, but there on the sofa, where Jason had been sitting, was the *New York Times* interview with Anita Bryant, describing how her anti-homosexual campaign she had begun in 1977 had affected her health, family, and career. That interview was seven months old. Jason had obviously kept it around.

"I wonder if she knows how her campaign has affected Jason and others like him," said Marta.

Then I saw, peeking out from underneath the newspaper, the corner of my missing blue journal. I reached down, picked it up, and slipped it into my shoulder bag. Marta saw me do it. She pretended she didn't.

Waiting for the police to arrive, we looked around in Jason's bathroom. The shattered mirror and blood on the counter explained the bandages on Jason's hands. It wasn't too hard to imagine that Jason couldn't bear his own reflection.

"Jason must have known they would come after him sooner or later," said Marta.

"Who? They?"

"I don't know. Maybe the voices inside his head."

FOURTEEN—EMILY'S TRUTH

After what Jason did to himself, Emily couldn't face her friends at the newspaper. She stayed home in Brystal Beach to read and write in the blue journal, now back in her possession:

> *All day that same old guilt has trailed behind me like a dog beholden to its owner. I shoo it away, pondering the irony in how there was a time when I thought Jason was faithful and that I was the miscreant, the one with the double life, even though it was a fantasy. It seemed amusing to me now, the time when I believed Jason truly loved me. Before I knew about Jason's double life, I wrote: I have, in agony, cursed this longing for another love as damnable, evil, and wished it were gone—only to later feel shame that I could deny so beautiful a gift.*

And Jason had read that.

Before I found out the truth, I thought that not just the men but also the women who knew Jason seemed to share intimacy with him that defied logic. Why did he seem so open with others, yet closed to me?

I told Marta that I would swear he was sleeping with half the town if I did not know better. But I thought I did know better. Before he was arrested, I thought Jason was faithful. Old faithful Jason. True-blue-good-as-gold-and-just-a-sweetheart-of-a-guy Jason. And I'm a rat. I once believed many women would kill for a husband like Jason.

Once, when I went on a diet, he washed my vegetables! Then when I was too sick to walk to the bathroom, he picked me up and carried me. He fed me, bathed me, and sat holding my hand for hours while I slept. I thought Jason loved me. That is why I felt so guilty about leaving him.

Jason loved me in his way. But that is not the point. Did I ever love him? Not in the way I love Alessio. Jason's double life was no fantasy. His was real, long before mine became real.

I suddenly feel justified in never loving Jason truly. Let the irony wash my guilt away. But my dream about being murdered by the jackal will not leave me.

Jason must have ben hurt terribly.

Again she turned to the dream:

I was drowning. It was as though I was under water in a big bucket or shallow well. I could see light shining down, or I was looking up through the water at light, I'm not sure which. A man's face appeared above me. He just stood there, leering at me. The water covered my head only by a few feet. I could see him, and he could see me. We just stared at each other. At first, the man appeared to be dark-skinned. Not black. More brown, like a Mexican. But as I stared up through the water at him, he sprouted fangs and dog-ears. His face started twisting and elongating into an evil-looking mass, and he laughed a hideous laugh, and he held my head underwater until I drowned.

(end of dream)

That was all there was to the dream, but it left me wary and apprehensive for days afterward. The dream maybe recurred twice a year for all of this life.

I spoke with Marta about how I had never learned to swim because I couldn't put my face under water. I also had this inexplicable fear of heights. Glass elevators always freaked me out, and once, visiting California, I stepped out onto a rock that overhung the Pacific and just started screaming as though I were falling. I worked to get over the fear in my mind and thought I was over it. Then one day at home, lying on my own sofa, I was watching Barefoot in the Park on TV. Robert Redford crawled out onto a skylight, and my knees turned to jelly right there on the sofa. I realized my mind understood there was nothing to fear, but my body hadn't gotten the message. It was as though the cells of my body—my knees in particular—remembered falling, not imagined, but remembered. Other times watching TV, a scene showing someone high up on a beam or something else high up, I've felt my stomach turn. Fear of heights and water.

"I wish I understood."

The sound of her own voice startled her.

FIFTEEN—JASON'S PSYCHIATRIST

Jason had been hospitalized for a week when Emily got a call requesting a meeting with Dr. Brant, Jason's psychiatrist.

She was still legally his wife. Wives—even almost ex-wives—get called to hospitals. She telephoned Marta to ask her to meet up afterward.

Even at two in the afternoon, the hospital corridor's eeriness made her feel as though the long white fluorescent tubes were his eyes, watching her. The jackal was out there, somewhere. She could feel it. Anyone observing her walk the long passageway would know from the way she rubbed her neck that it burned, but that she was only vaguely aware of it.

She carried the look of a woman concerned, yet resigned to accept whatever she had to. Her eyes appeared to be both sad and determined. This, too, would pass, wouldn't it?

The worn, waxed, asphalt tiles made her shoes klip-klop. She followed the yellow tiles flanked by green. The windowless walls were painted pink—a shiny, beigey pink that reflected the slightest shadows, enough to give her a sense of movement. She realized that if she could see herself moving along the walls and could hear her shoes klip klop, she must be walking. Otherwise, she was stoically calm, permitting herself to feel only the same apprehension and uncertainty she would feel in any difficult situation.

Black letters on the two white locked doors ahead were becoming readable:

PSYCHIATRIC INTENSIVE CARE UNIT. NO ADMITTANCE.

Emily reasoned they would permit her to enter, as the doctor had called and requested she meet him there. Some questions, he had said.

Walking along, behind her she heard a *crunchklunk*. She stopped and listened for the sound again. Warm waves of panic surged upward, slid from the floor up her back, shrouded her head for a moment like a hood, then cascaded forward and downward, washing all her masks away.

The sound of soft footsteps informed her someone was behind her, walking toward her, wearing sneakers of some sort, not street shoes.

And wheels. She could hear wheels rolling. If he were coming to kill her, he wouldn't be pushing . . . an orderly. Pushing a wheelchair, or a rolling bed.

"Mornin'," the orderly smiled and spoke as he passed, an unconscious patient strapped onto his cart. Emily nodded a reciprocal greeting, embarrassed that this stranger had witnessed her fear. Straightening, she realized she had been leaning against the wall, half expecting these to be the last moments of her life. This life anyway.

She paused to adjust the Irish-crème silk jacket of her tunic suit. She smoothed the skirt and ran her right index finger underneath the belt, grabbed the buckle and yanked centerward. The dreams had been affecting her sleep, and she had lost weight, making her clothes looser.

The orderly had pushed a button when he had reached the white doors. They had opened and swallowed him and his charge. In a moment, they would swallow Emily. She looked down at her feet and realized they hurt. She'd never have worn sling-back high heels had she known the corridor was the yellow-brick road straight into the valley of the shadow of death.

A voice said, *Don't mix your metaphors, Emily. Remember who you are.*

Yes, and truth is stranger than fiction, she said right back.

No clichés, please, said the voice.

Shut up, please, Emily answered. Then the buzzer was beneath her finger.

Gone was the numbness that had enabled her to come this far, and she was left at the mercy of her raging senses. Screams were coming from behind the doors, which, when opened, thrust forth the smell of sickness and death mingled with Lysol.

"This way to Dr. Brant's office," a nurse said, apparently oblivious to the screams.

Emily was relieved that it was not Jason's voice.

Just inside the doors, beigey-pink paint gave way to white, a bluish, deathly white, a horrible, shiny, easy-to-wipe-the-blood-off white. Emily was surprised not to see blood anywhere. She now had Jason connected with spurting blood, but before she could sort it out, the doctor spoke, and she realized she was standing in his office, dazed.

He said, "Thank you for coming, Mrs. Wohl. I'm Dr. Brant, and I've been assigned to your husband's case."

"May I close your door, Doctor?" she asked, politely, but rather firmly.

She could not hear herself think amidst the screams.

"Of course. Sorry," he said.

Emily closed the door and, feeling faint, plopped down in a chair across from his messy desk.

Now, Mrs. Wohl," he said, leaning back in his large black executive chair, "we're a little confused as to just what brought Jason to us in this condition."

An ambulance, of course. But she did not say that.

"How is he?" she said instead.

"We think he will live," he said comfortingly, as though he assumed Emily would be relieved.

Which is not at all the right assumption, but I don't feel like getting into it with him as it is none of his business why I am divorcing Jason anyway, and Alessio is waiting for me, and could we please just get this over with, I'm just here doing the Christian thing, expressing concern for a fellow human being who has done a terrible thing to himself, but it has nothing to do with me, I'm just a witness to Jason's perversion, I did nothing to cause it.

"But he has lost the sight in that eye," the doctor continued. "In fact, we had to remove it."

Emily's mind stopped racing.

"Removed Jason's eye? What do you want to know, Doctor?"

"We'd like to know why you think he did this to himself."

Because I saw him do it, of course.

"Because he couldn't stand to look at me." Emily watched his face, carefully as he placed all ten fingertips together, pondering her answer. Rising from his chair and walking around to the front of his desk, he towered over her, obviously trying to intimidate her.

Finally he said, "Are you saying you drove him

to it?"

Leaning back in her chair and peering up into the doctor's accusing eyes, Emily tried to see him as he was seeing her.

His dark-rimmed glasses magnified already slightly bulging eyes. His forehead extended all the way to the back of his head to the crease where his skull met the back of his neck. A little ring of dark curls wrapped around to meet graying, bushy sideburns, the only other hair on his head. He was large and tall, and stood with both hands in the pockets of his white jacket, rocking back and forth on his heels, a habit he no doubt developed while trying to appear casual whenever he wasn't saying all that he knew. He probably thought wives mustn't be told too much too soon. Even soon-to-be ex-wives.

"I don't know anymore, Doctor, who drove whom to what. Regardless, I am no longer Jason's wife except in name only, and that will be legalized soon. The divorce papers were filed before Jason was hospitalized. No court will delay the proceedings."

Emily left Brant's office exhausted from having to defend herself to this entirely unappealing fellow, whom she instantly mistrusted. That, plus the fear she had been feeling, had only amplified in his presence, and she did not know why.

Outside in the hospital parking lot, fumbling for

her keys, Emily felt the hair rise on the back of her neck.

He's here. He has been waiting for me. I will not be paralyzed with fright as I was in that corridor.

She glanced over her right shoulder, then her left, checking the cars in the lot. Seeing no one who resembled the jackal in her dream, she unlocked the Jaguar and slid inside. She set the mirrors so she could see all around and behind her and locked the doors, just in case. She started the engine and turned on the air conditioning, seeking relief from the mid-June heat, but left the radio off. She needed to think.

Dr. Brant's words came rushing back . . . "Don't expect too much too soon . . . long-term illness . . . must have seen it coming on . . . .

The bullet smashed through the driver's side window.

SIXTEEN—JASON'S VOICES

Humboldt Brant, M.D., slid his dark-rimmed glasses downward on his nose and rubbed the crease in his neck, then fingered his little ring of dark curls as he read what Jason had written at his insistence. He had himself put in charge of monitoring Jason since the incident that put him into the Water's Edge Hospital Psychiatric Unit, even though Jason was not mentally ill. He was, rather, emotionally ill, so much so as to be a danger to himself.

> My name is Jason Wohl. I've been hospitalized since June 9th, and the doctors want to know why I did this to myself. I shall try to tell them.
>
> It started that day almost exactly a year ago.
>
> The approaching sunset drew me like a magnet out of the last century toward the beach. I liked to leave the newspaper I

owned and drive out across the Causeway to Shell Key. This day I parked at the Westin and walked the beach to the jetty, where tourists on party boats navigating the channel deliriously oohed and aahed over every seagull perched on every piling. They waved madly to me, as though they had to share their joy in being there. I waved back, smiling wanly, briefly letting myself feel their sadness at having to go home.

Home. I no longer have a home.

The tide was low, and sea worm casings littered the golden alabaster sand. High and dry starfish patiently awaited the Gulf of Mexico's return. Sunset at low tide. It made me feel the earth, resting from the morning storm. I drank with my eyes the oranges, pinks and lavenders no artist's brush could ever paint because the colors wouldn't hold still long enough to be captured. I watched the big golden ball melt into the horizon and pretended I could hear it sizzle as the ocean doused its light.

Would Emily come home that night? Or any night?

Once upon a mind there was a problem to which there was no solution.

Disembodied voices chanted inside my head. `Yah yah, yah yah, yah yah. Em i le ee kn ow s!'

The childish cadence drummed through my numb brain, and I wished I were a starfish waiting to be swept out to sea by a merciful tide. Emily was in Fort Lauderdale. With him.

Before she found him, I read her journal. She would never write with such passion about me.

Emily was looking for a lost lover. I had found mine.

Being with Alfredo the night before seemed unreal as I watched Emily's beautiful, delicate body sprawled nude before me in childlike sleep. I sagged under the dreaded weight in my head. I closed my eyes to the vision as I observed her. She must never know. Never.

My usually orderly mind scanned my morning schedule, but the sight of her— and my guilt— erased my itinerary from my mind. My fist clenched, resisting touching her. I was torn between my need to gather her in my arms and beg forgiveness and my need to run. Rising passion pushed last evening's episode to the left of here and now, opening space in my mind to focus on the reality of the moment. Emily's beauty.

The bulge was spoiling the pleat in my pants. I stepped into her closet. The fragrance of Isadora floated through her simple silk dresses. I touched her baggy linen trousers, knowing she had no idea how sexy she looked in these. Her jewel case, almost empty except for four diamond ear studs, two carats each for her double-pierced ears, my wedding gift to her. Why did I ever marry her? Because she's irresistible, that's why. And because I thought with her I would be normal. The journal was under her jewel case.

Holding Emily's journal in my hands I could almost feel its secrets. There was no question whether I would read it. It was as though my guilt compelled me. I looked at her again, the soft curve of her spine, left knee drawn under her, punctuated by two deep dimples where her hips and buttocks join, tanned, slender legs, tousled dark hair, and flawless skin, glowing like the blue satin sheets on which she lay. The sight of her made my hands tingle, and I wanted to bury my face in her body, it didn't matter where.

But my tingling hands were holding her journal. I wished she would turn over so I could see the pubescent breasts I'd loved for what seemed like a hundred years. Then I opened it and started to read:

I look inside my mind, and I see you

I look inside my soul, and I see you

You're blocking my view

I reach inside the blackness, the darkest place in me, the most unholy thoughts I can think, and you are there.

I turn to face the light, the brightest place in me, the most holy thoughts I can think, and you are there.

Your eyes are watching me. I can see them.

Your lips are kissing me. I can taste them.

Your hands are touching me. I can feel them.

Why can't I have you again?

I knew she wasn't writing about me. She described sexual desires I didn't know she possessed. How could I blame her? As beautiful and desirable as she was, and even though I responded to her physically as a man, my fantasies all centered on Alfredo.

This peculiar infidelity. To yearn and burn for a man, in a dingy motel in a filthy room with a sink in the corner and a bare light bulb overhead. I don't go there to make love. Love plays no part in my secret life.

I wretched, picturing her face if she ever knew. How can I touch her with the same hands that…And now she knows.

Some stories never end. I hope I never get out of this hospital. Maybe here I am safe from myself. Maybe Emily is safe from me. They say my eye . . . .

A psychedelic haze flashed through my mind, and in the moment before darkness overtook me, I saw huge tears coming toward me. Giant goblets of sadness, with faces, arms, legs, and lives of their own, dancing, menacingly shaking their fists and wailing, 'Why, Jason, why have you denied us?' And I knew these were the tears I had never cried and would never cry now that the eye that contained them was gone.

Dr. Brant placed Jason's tablet on the desk and started to pull off his glasses just as Nurse Achi burst into his office, excitedly disclosing, "Emily Wohl has been shot. She's downstairs in emergency."
Brant left his glasses on, the better to hide his smile.

SEVENTEEN—EMILY'S ENEMY

Alfredo Gonzales scraped his fingernails through his greasy black mop with one hand and rubbed his round hairy belly with the other. Ten years ago he'd driven the first yellow Cadillac Jason had bought him into Tampa Bay. He'd left a suicide note in the glove compartment of the car addressed to Jason. But he'd written it with a dark blue felt tip pen that smeared when it hit the water so no one could read what it said:

What did you have for a *mamasito*, Jason? Mine is Satan's wife.

The paramedics pulled him out of the bay before he drowned and thought the incident an accident. Alfredo decided destiny was on his side—

maybe brother Archibald was right—so he kept his mouth shut and waited, determined never to be that weak again.

Alfredo paid the two-day hospital bill with dried out cash Jason had given him, fished out of the glove compartment. The dumb broad admitting clerk hadn't asked for ID since he was paying in cash. The cops had nothing on him then, so they ignored him when he caught a cab back to Tampa to wait for Jason's call, which he knew would come. Jason's calls always came.

This yellow Cadillac was the third one Jason had bought him

Jason had only been in the hospital two weeks, and the money was already drying up. He couldn't let that happen. He'd have to call brother Archibald, or maybe brother Brant. He's a shrink. Almost as much money as a preacher.

Anyway, *mamasito* was holding out. Said she wouldn't give him any more money until that Emily broad was dead.

Guess it is time.

He pulled the high-powered rifle out of the box at the end of his bed and loaded it. He checked the scope and headed out the door to climb to the roof of Water's Edge Hospital, where he knew he'd have a clear shot.

Brother Brant will call Emily to the hospital. She will go. I will be there.

EIGHTEEN—DEATH BY RUMOUR

The short distance elongated before Marta like a stretched out rubber band, twisting underneath her as she tried to keep her equilibrium from surrendering completely to the grief overtaking her as she stumbled back to where Emily lay slumped in the driver's seat of her car. Blood oozed from Emily's head. She was supposed to meet Emily to hear how it went with Brant.

"My God, my God, sweet Jesus, help me," Marta cried out, loudly enough to be heard by patrons gathering in the hospital doorway, alarmed by the sound of gunfire disturbing the usually tranquil setting of the hospital. One of them hurried back inside to call the police. Marta collapsed onto her knees to reach Emily inside the Jaguar, afraid to touch her without knowing exactly how much damage the bullet has done to Emily's head. Her police training kicked in, and she felt Emily's pulse. Still strong, but Emily was unconscious.

Marta looked across the parking lot, then up at the roof of the hospital. No gunman in sight but that had to be where he was. She took off her jacket and laid it gently across Emily, then, with her fingers, gingerly parted Emily's shiny brown hair where blood was seeping through. She gently inspected the entry and exit wounds, relieved to see the bullet probably just grazed Emily's skull. She calculated the trajectory of the bullet.

To the first officer on the scene she said, yanking out her ID, "Get some men on the roof. The shot came from there."

"Yes, Miss Miller. Right away," the officer replied, then ran to his squad car to call for detectives.

"Get Mandino," Marta shouted. "Tell him I think the Christionologists did this."

Attendants rushed out with a gurney and carefully lifted Emily out of her car. In the emergency room, Marta held Emily's small hand, praying and cursing, cursing and praying

"I've been cussin' and prayin' ever since this case began," she said to no one in particular.

"She'll be all right, Miss Miller," one of them answered. "Her vital signs are strong. But she probably has a concussion. She may be out for awhile."

Inside the hospital, Marta paced the yellow tiles flanked by green, waiting for Alessio to arrive. The drive across Tampa Bay from the *Tampa Chronicle* shouldn't take more than half an hour, as the traffic should not be all that bad at two-thirty in the afternoon, Marta reasoned.

Marta listened outside the door to Nurse Stanton's babbling.

Inside the shiny white procedures room, prep nurse Corey Stanton shaved Emily's head and jabbered merrily away, out loud, in her Scottish brogue, as if Emily could hear her.

"Just look at this shiny hair. Did you ever see prettier? Shame to shave it all off. I could always cut only half, but you little darlins' always end up shaving it all anyway, so it'll not grow out all cockeyed and all. Wish I had hair like yours. And look at your sweet skin, all freckly and fresh. Why, you look like a child. The chart says you're 34, but you surely don't look it, what, not with that body. Wish I had a body like yours, all slender and cute. Even your precious little bubbies look like a young girl. You're very feminine looking, like a ballerina you are. My, my, what a shame."

"Nurse, is the patient prepped?" asked Dr. Witherspoon, sternly, accustomed to the portly nurse's benevolent ramblings, even if the patient can't hear her.

"Sorry, Doctor. She's all yours," said the nurse, and she stood by respectfully while he examined Emily's head wound.

Marta fidgeted silently outside the exam room, wishing he would hurry.

After he had finished his exam, Dr. Witherspoon came out of the exam room in time to see Alessio striding down the hallway, head jutting forward, long powerful arms reaching out to Marta for a hug before stoically taking his place beside her, arm around her shoulder, to listen to his report on Emily's condition. It would be any bystander's guess who was holding up whom.

"Mrs. Wohl has suffered a trauma to the brain. We don't think it is severe. The bullet only grazed her skull," he said in that clipped manner doctors use when they simply do not know. "There is some swelling, but we don't think it is serious. My only concern is we don't know why she is in a coma. She should come out of it soon, but we never know with a head injury just how long it will take."

Marta and Alessio gazed at each other tenderly. Any bystander would see how they were bonded in their love for Emily and in their ferocious determination to find justice.

"Jason's involved in this somehow," Marta said.

"How could he be? He's been upstairs in the psychiatric ward for weeks," replied Alessio, extracting his arm from Marta's shoulder.

"I don't know how, but my gut knows that he is. My gut is never wrong." Her voice broke. Marta stepped back and looked down at the floor.

"I know better than to doubt you. Emily says you are usually right about most things. How can I help?" Alessio said. He reached out and pulled her to him. She touched her forehead to his chest, trying to hide her tears.

"I don't know yet, but with Emily out of commission, I'll need you. I'll order a guard at her door until we can get her moved.

"Doctor, please help us put out the story that she died. We don't want anybody to know he nearly missed, except Eddy. We can tell Eddy."

"Of course," said Dr. Witherspoon.

"Done," said Alessio. "And don't worry. I will not leave her side."

He disentangled himself from Marta to go call the newspapers to put out the story that Emily was dead. It was the only way to protect her.

NINETEEN—AGNES' BIG CHANCE

Agnes Sandors, managing editor of the *Sawgrass Prism,* a weekly ad rag that kept the community informed about who died and who got arrested, was redheaded, skinny and bowlegged, with a fat belly, a missing tooth and a dirty neck. But Marta knew she would get more information out of her than she could the local cops.

Country cops dislike city slickers moving in on their turf, and anybody from down there in Pineapple County was a city slicker to them. However, a cow pasture editor would be flattered by the attention, Marta hoped. Especially this one. Marta had heard that Agnes Sandors fancied herself a Woodward and Bernstein waiting for something to happen in her territory.

This is your big chance, Marta thought to herself, sitting in Sandors' office, observing how different this woman was from Emily.

Brittle eyes. Hardened from being passed over by life. Sad.

If Emily would only wake up and get well.

"What brings you here?" Sandors asked, peering out over the top of spectacles not meant to be worn at the end of her bulbous nose, which was peppered with blackheads.

Marta tried to ignore the dirty ring around the woman's neck and focus on why she was there.

"I need your help," Marta said.

"*Eh?*" Sandors answered, and Marta detected a distinctive Canadian twang in her voice, Marta decided was a good thing because it probably meant she was an outsider and unlikely to be one of the bad guys. Maybe it said she could be trusted a bit more than she could if she'd grown up in a Sawgrass County trailer park with a Klansman father and a cauldron-stirring witch for a grandmother. Most of the mothers in these places had been so physically abused by their husbands that they ran off and left the kids with the grandmothers.

"My colleague and best friend, Emily Mason-Wohl, a columnist at the *Water's Edge Daily News*, was shot a week ago today. You must keep this confidential, but she is still in a coma at Water's Edge Hospital," said Marta.

"*Eh?* I heard she died," said Agnes Sandors.

"Yes, and that's the story we have to stick to. We were working together on something that was pointing us in this direction. We'd heard of a cult called the Christionologists operating a farm up this way. We think they're part of that herd of automatons down in Water's Edge, the one's headed up by the Reverend Archibald T. Angler."

Agnes leaned backward in her chair and crossed her hands across her bloated belly, peering still, glints flashing, gray coals glowing in her eyes. She smelled a story.

"Where was she when she was shot?"

"In the parking lot of the Water's Edge Hospital."

"Daylight? Witnesses?"

"None so far. I'm the closest thing to a witness. I was in the parking lot when she was shot, but I didn't get a look at the gunman."

"Might be scared. I've heard those Christionologists are a scary lot."

"Who said that?"

"I read," Agnes answered, a tad sarcastically Marta thought, but then she was willing to cut Agnes some slack, at least until she found a reason not to.

"Here's what we know so far. We have known for a long time that Angler's so-called television ministry called Christionology is connected somehow to a cult of devil worshippers up here in Sawgrass."

"I tell you right quick, if this pans out, I want an

exclusive," Agnes's voice crackled with excitement.

"It's not mine to give, but with Emily out I'll put you ahead of the line, as long as Eddy gets everything you know, too."

"Done," said Agnes. "I hear Angler preaching on TV, no more suffering, no more poverty, sickness, or death if you give him enough money. It's enough to make ya sick, yes it is."

A dark shadow lightly crossed Marta's field of inner vision. It was all she required to grasp the mirrored, hideous truth of Angler's vitriolic truculence.

"We have a witness to his having sex with a minor, but that's the problem. She's a minor. She has been helpful with information about babies being stolen from hospitals all over the country. They plant cult members in delivery rooms then choose babies of poor young mothers without husbands or family who might investigate. They say the babies have been cremated. By accident. They get away with it because the mothers have no contact with anyone other than their nurses and doctors."

"They have to have a doctor in their pocket. Easy to do because of shortages," said Agnes. "A nurse, too."

"Gotta be a doctor signing the death certificates, but who is handing the babies out the back door?" said Marta.

"What's their reason to steal children?" said Agnes.

"We think they are training them for sex when they get to be about three or four years old."

"You mean something like that is going on right here in Sawgrass County, Florida?" Agnes' face got redder, and she snatched off her glasses in disbelief, threw them on the desk, got up out of her chair, and started pacing.

"The paper put a man inside undercover to find out the truth about Angler. He was discovered. They have printed stories about me, trying to ruin me, and now they have tried to kill Emily because she writes editorials about them."

Agnes Sandors' police radio went off.

"Shots fired out on Palmetto Road . . . ."

TWENTY—GOOBEY THE HERO

The group gathered in the darkened room, surrounded by candles made of black wax in the shape of huge penises, black wax cats, chicken feathers, and beads of colored plastic. Books on séances, devil worship, communicating with the dark side, black magic, pagan rituals, human sacrifice, sexual slavery, and every perverse, sordid cruel inhuman thing one human being can do to another, lined the shelves.

Three men and two women chanted, *Uturuncu Duppy. Uturuncu Duppy. Uturuncu Duppy.*

They all wore small golden foxes on chains around their necks. They were a remnant of an ancient sect that worshipped Utu, the Sumerian Sun God, the counterpart of the Akkadian Shamash, his satanic majesty.

The high priestess had decided. Tomorrow

Roarsh would snatch the next neonate. Roarsh was old and could be trusted not to mutilate the infant for his own pleasure as Ob had done.

Alfredo would exterminate the Marta bitch as he had Emily Wohl. Holly would be brought back to the farm and killed, but they'd have to hide it from Granny K.

No, Alfredo didn't want the girl first. He liked men and animals. Goobey was too stupid to know what to do with her. Just kill her and get it over with.

"But I like her, Mumsy," the Reverend Archibald T. Angler said to the high priestess.

"Don't argue with our mother, Brother Dear," Alfredo answered, sliding low in his chair, waiting for the blow on the head to come from the high priestess. Instead, a door opened, and Goobey, holding Granny K's Uzi, opened fire on the group. When he was done, everyone lay dead.

TWENTY-ONE—CHRIONS DEFEATED

Saturday afternoon, Marta spread the newspaper out on Emily's rumpled hospital bed and started reading. Emily opened her eyes and smiled at Marta, letting her know she was awake and paying attention. She had awakened while Marta was in Agnes Sandors' office the day before. Alessio had filled her in as much as he knew.

The masthead showed the date, Saturday, June 24, 1979. Eddy himself wrote the story.

Cult leader massacred
by Edward Monroe

SAWGRASS—The Reverend Archibald T. Angler, 50, founder of Christionology was murdered Friday in a bloody massacre that included several family members. Victims included two half-brothers, Humboldt T. Brant, M.D., 48, and Alfredo Gonzales and twin sister Achi Consuelo, 50. Their mother, Angel Ramirez, 72, also was killed. Police said the group was originally from St. Louis, MO, but had relocated to Water's Edge, where Angler's ministry established their headquarters. The farm where the murders occurred is located in on Palmetto Road in Sawgrass County.

Sawgrass County Sheriff Department deputies took suspect Gerald (Goobey) Garner, 29, into custody, after he confessed at the scene and surrendered an Uzi, legally registered to Karen Matthews, 68, of Sawgrass County. The Uzi is famous for being an open bolt, blowback-operated submachine gun, used by Israeli Special Forces.

Mrs. Matthews said she kept the gun for personal protection. "I did not know Goobey knew I had it," she told investigators, saying she kept the gun underneath a chair in her room at the farm, believed to be an assisted living facility for church members. Mrs. Matthews said the gun had never been fired as far as she knew.

Collected as evidence at the crime scene

was an assortment of pornographic materials that included wax figures associated with the occult. Chrion officials disavowed any knowledge of involvement with practices such as the items suggested. Investigators are questioning residents at the farm where the murders occurred.

Garner told police his motive for the killings was to protect a young woman he loves, Holly Smith, and to avenge the attack on newspaper woman, Emily Mason, who was shot in the Water's Edge Hospital parking lot June 22. A cover story saying she was deceased circulated for her protection. Garner is cooperating with police and offered to testify against remaining members of the cult, which, he claims, is nationwide. He is expected to be arraigned Monday morning at the Sawgrass County Courthouse.

"Oh, my, it's worse than we thought," said Emily

"My one regret is that I can't prosecute," said Marta. "It happened in the wrong county."

"I'd say count your blessings. This has been a long time coming. Can't you just hear the weeping and wailing and gnashing of teeth in the Angler camp. I just feel sorry for those poor people who gave him money."

"An old professor of mine used to say 'people can't get themselves into more trouble than they deserve'," said Marta. "And I'm certain we can come up with something illegal in this county. We could have gotten Angler with Holly's testimony, but now he's dead."

Alessio came into Emily's room, sauntered over to her bedside and smiled at Marta as he bent down to kiss Emily's bald head. "My lips feel prickles," he said.

Emily put her hand on her head. "Oh no. I'm bald. I'll need a wig."

Together Alessio and Marta shouted, "*No!*"

One said, "You look adorable."

The other said, "What you need is a sexy tattoo that will always be there, invisible, under your hair."

"Got one. Been there already." Emily carefully fingered the bandage covering the bullet wound. "He must have been a bad shot."

"Well, he was on the roof, and your car window was up. He did not see you clearly."

"Thank God."

"My car! Where is my car? Did I bleed all over it?"

"It is in Impound. It's evidence."

"No problem," said Alessio, eyes twinkling at his surprise.

"How do you feel, *Luv*?" said Marta.

Emily appeared to be thinking it over. *I like it when she calls me 'Luv.'*

"I don't feel guilty anymore. And I'm ready to get out of here."

"They are signing your release papers now. I have a surprise—no, two surprises—waiting for you at home."

Marta's face lit up because she knew that one was a new white Jaguar, and the other was the latest Apple II PLUS computer to replace her old typewriter on which she had written the story about Brenda.

TWENTY-TWO—THE WRAPUP

Sunday afternoon, Emily inhaled the balmy breeze floating in through the open sliding glass door, glad for no rustling papers or paperweights.

The black computer screen began to fill with green letters:

> After the Mexican had thrown me off the cliff, I needed a rest, so I did not reincarnate until the century was about to change. During Prohibition in Chicago, I, Emily Abigail Mason-Wohl, was a hooker named Ruby. Jason was a small-time thug named Arnie.
>
> I had frowsy red hair until flappers came into style. Then I cut it stylishly short. Arnie hung around the edges of the Capone gang, drooling over their money and cars.
>
> He tried to get me to give up "the life" and marry him. But even though I didn't

consciously recall what happened in Chetco when we were Brenda and Bond, some part of me knew I wasn't about to make that mistake again. I think I tortured him, flaunting myself with other men. I instinctively distrusted him. Besides, he was a wimp. I did not have to remember on a conscious level. The soul never forgets. This explains why I was born feeling guilty. The soul never forgets these things.

I also know that after I had died as Brenda, Aunt Jessee died of syphilis. I am glad I did not have to watch that. It would have hit her brain within ten years—twenty if she was lucky. I also know that after my death, Bond never cried. Jason's eye? Of course.

I know too that Aunt Jessee must have known she was going to die. That must be why she pushed me into marrying Bond. She was devoted to me, but she was so determined to find me a suitable husband she must have known she would not be around to bail me out if I needed it. She had been so afraid I would either fall in love with a shipwrecked sailor or a sea captain or worse, set out on my own for San Francisco. She would have had a fit if she had seen me as Ruby. She would have blamed herself because she had been a hooker in her youth. In New York, she had been known as the Madam of Fifth Avenue. She probably would have approved of my being cynical and street-smart, too smart to be dominated by one man.

However, as Ruby I was not even first-class as Jessee had been in New York. I sat around on a barstool, with my two little dogs waiting at my feet for me to find a mark. The fur babies had learned to wait quietly on the floor by the bed while I worked. My regulars knew they were part of the package and did not complain.

As Ruby, I did not want to marry, or to have children, after what had happened to Jenny. I never did find her again. Nor did I find Alessio, or Emil, as he called himself in Chetco.

After the Mexican murdered me, he never returned to Chetco, so Emil did not know what had happened to me. No one had seen the Mexican knock on my door, so he never was caught.

The Mexican did not show up in Chicago either, but that did not stop me from being killed again. As Bond, he meant to kill me. As Arnie, he did not mean to but he got me killed anyway. I suppose that should make me feel better.

When I was killed in Chicago, it was the dead of winter. Blowing snow and wind, freezing, wet air froze in your lungs and made you feel like you were drowning. It made me want to stay in my apartment over the bar this particular night. Arnie knocked on my door, uninvited—he was always unwanted and unwelcome—but that never stopped him. The dogs were so accustomed to his knock they did not even bark. I opened the door, and there he stood, hat in hand, his brown overcoat speckled with snow and ice that was melting, leaving wet spots that looked like dirt.

Arnie was strange. He always appeared bedraggled no matter how he was dressed, but the main thing that strikes me now about him is that he always looked as though he needed to cry, but couldn't or wouldn't. Now I understand.

I let the little twerp in, as always, dope that I was. He whimpered something about how he had to talk to me, to try to convince me to let him spend the rest of his life taking care of me. Ha! The joke turned out to be on him since his life ended that very night. But then so did mine.

I argued with him for awhile, then told

him to leave. He refused, saying he wanted to stay the night. I let other guys stay the night, why not him. I decided I would never be rid of him if I did not ask him to take me downstairs for a drink or something. Booze was illegal, but then so was prostitution. In that neighborhood, a little thing like a law never mattered much.

I lied and promised Arnie I might let him come back up with me if he would buy me a drink first. I would have said anything to get him out of there.

Downstairs, the crowd was light, but in the corner sat a man who oozed so much money it's a wonder I had not smelled him from the apartment above. I could always spot the rich ones.

Anyway, I knew he was out of his territory because I knew the face of every man who belonged in that bar, and he didn't. Sure enough, a car pulled up outside, and one of Capone's thugs started blasting one of those "Tommy guns" they used back then. Arnie and I both got caught in the crossfire right where we stood. And that was that.

I just know I would not have been standing there if it had not been for trying to get rid of Arnie.

I never did know who took care of the dogs. I had named one of my dogs Jessee, the other, Jenny. But I didn't remember why. Now I remember.

Alessio came in off the deck, saw Emily enjoying her new computer, then turned around and headed back out, where he was tending the grill, getting it ready for steaks. He wished Eddy had not invited himself out today. Eddy used the excuse their need to bring in a new publisher for the paper, but Alessio knew he just wanted to see for himself that she was all right. *Eddy loves her too.* The wall phone rang.

"If that is Marta, ask her to come and have steak with us. Tell her to bring Ham," said Emily.

"Hello," said Alessio.

"How's our girl?"

"Hammering away. She wants you to come for steaks and bring Ham."

"That might be a little awkward," Marta mumbled. "Erich and I are at the beach already."

Emily overheard Alessio say, "Erich?"

"Tell her Detective Mandino is welcome."

"I heard her," said Marta. She turned around in time to see Erich Jasper Mandino nod in agreement.

"We'll be there," she said.

Alessio heard Emily open a drawer and papers rattle behind him. Emily was swishing a stapled sheath of typewriter paper in the air. "I have something here for you to read."

"What is it?"

"Just a little story I wrote the day of the Yo-Yo Ma concert."

"The day we met."

He took the sheath.

"What is it about?"

"You read it and tell me. I think it's about us."

Alessio frowned as he read the first line.

"I remember being murdered."

The End

TIMELINE FOR *LOVE OF MY LIVES*

1811 – 1865 New York, Oregon

- Emily's story about her past life as Brenda.

1978 Florida

- October 27, Emily meets Alessio
- November 11, Emily and Alessio in St. Petersburg Beach hotel
- November 13, Jason is missing, but he returns; Emily tells him she is leaving.

1979 Florida

- May 25, Jason is arrested; Marta gets a call from Holly, offering to help
- May 26, Story runs in Tampa paper
- May 31, Emily and Marta meet Holly at Jack's
- June 9, Jason calls Emily to the condo.
- June 15, Emily is called to hospital and is shot.
- June 22, Marta goes to Sawgrass to meet with Agnes. Goobey wipes out the villains. Emily wakes up.
- June 24, Story runs in paper. Emily leaves hospital. Goes home to Brystal Beach.

WHO WAS WHOM

- Emily Mason-Wohl was Brenda Callahan
- Jason Wohl was Bond Bartello
- Alessio Giles Lavalle was Emil Chevalier
- Marta Miller was Jessee McClannahan O'Riley
- Holly Smith was Alice O'Riley, Jessee's daughter who died
- Edward (Eddy) Monroe was Jim Johnstone
- Alfredo Gonzalez was Jose, the noxious Mexican
- The other Christionologists were the family Bond Bartello rescued from the fire in St. Louis, proving "no good deed goes unpunished."

Contact me online: www.RiverDaniel.com

Or email: 99RiverDaniel@gmail.com

Love of My Lives is available in print as an ebook on Amazon.

Also, you may enjoy *Suicide Angels: From Desperation to Restoration, Hope from the Other Side,* first published in June 2014. If you or someone you know has been touched by suicide, this book is a must-read. It is also available on Amazon in print and as an eBook.